AMERICA'S
SECRET DESTINY

AMERICA'S
SECRET DESTINY
Spiritual Vision & the Founding of a Nation

Robert Hieronimus, Ph.D.

Destiny Books,
Rochester, Vermont

Destiny Books
One Park Street
Rochester, Vermont 05767

Library of Congress Cataloging-in-Publication Data

Hieronimus, Robert
America's secret destiny : spiritual vision and the founding of a
nation / Robert R. Hieronimus.
p. cm.
Bibliography: p.
Includes index.
ISBN 0-89281-255-9 :
1. United States—Seal. 2. Occultism—United States—History-
-Miscellanea. 3. United States—History—Miscellanea. I. Title.
CD5610.H54 1989
973—dc20   89-16768
                                                                CIP

Text design by C.J. Petlick, Hunter Graphics.

Cover collage by Jim Harter.
Cover design by Leslie Phillips.

Printed and bound in the United States.

10 9 8 7 6 5 4 3 2

Destiny Books is a division of Inner Traditions International, Ltd.

Distributed to the book trade in the United States by
American International Distribution Corporation (AIDC)

Distributed to the book trade in Canada by Book Center, Inc.,
Montreal, Quebec.

Dedication

At my darkest hour entered a soul of light who turned tragedy into self fulfillment. Without Zoh M. Hieronimus this book would have remained in process. This work is dedicated to her—the flower of the universe in the garden of my heart.

About the Author

Robert R. Hieronimus received his Ph.D. for the doctoral thesis "An Historic Analysis of the Reverse of the American Great Seal and Its Relationship to the Ideology of Humanistic Psychology" at Saybrook Institute in 1981. Dr. Hieronimus's research on the Great Seal has been used in the speeches, literature, and libraries of the White House (1976, 1982), the State Department (1978), and the Department of Interior (1982). His Independence Hall speech on the Great Seal's bicentennial was published in the Congressional Record (1983, 1984), and his research was shared in a personal meeting with former Egyptian President Anwar El-Sadat. He and his wife, Zoh, have been lobbying the House and Senate on the Great Seal Act (1982–1986). Dr. Hieronimus is also the talk show host of 21st Century Radio. The Dr. Bob Show is aired on two radio networks, Atlantic Coast Radio and the American Radio Networks, which have over 200 affiliates. 21st Century Radio explores the unknown with the world's leading edge thinkers, researchers, and practitioners in such fields as parapsychology, holistic health, UFOs, and the environment.

Contents

Acknowledgments

Many have made this book possible. First among them is my wife, Zoh M. Hieronimus, to whom this work is dedicated. A glance at the afterword will tell you why. Laura Cortner typed and researched specific problems in the text. Other transcribers were Rebekah Grossman, Janet Kinne, and Lisa Burke.

My son, Michael, and daughters, Maré and Anna, patiently waited for their father's attention, and the spirits of Mrs. Mari H. Milholland, my late mother-in-law, Mrs. Lyn P. Meyerhoff, and "uncle" Thomas Galen Hieronymus provided important input.

My alma mater, Saybrook Institute, my doctoral committee adviser, Stanley Krippner, Ph.D., and outside reader, Willis Harman, Ph.D., were instrumental in guiding my doctoral studies upon which much of this book is based. This publication would not have taken its present form without their assistance. Many thanks also to "White Eagle."

Introduction

One day, while fondling one of my remaining dollar bills, I was utterly astonished to discover on the back the reverse or pyramid side of America's Great Seal. I was familiar with the Great Seal's obverse or eagle side, but the enigmatic pyramid and the eye in the triangle suspended above it proved to me how ignorant I really was about the nation I dearly love.

The symbols on the seal's reverse captured my attention and filled me with wonder. I wrote the State Department asking about its history and meaning. Their reply was a full-color folder on the seal's obverse that made no mention of the seal's other side. Thinking this an oversight, I inquired again. They responded with a black and white photograph of the seal's reverse with no explanation.

The Great Seal's reverse entered my life at a critical point. I saw America at that time as a disintegrating culture. To me, the imagery on the seal's less well-known side suggested a nation with a greater destiny than wars and hypocrisy. I was perplexed and disappointed at our government's apparent disinterest in this important symbol of our national purpose.

On my own, I soon found several works that fed my curiosity about the reverse's meaning and its mysterious origins. Some of these authors asserted that the seal's design had originated from secret societies: Freemasons, Rosicrucians, and Illuminati. For these writers the seal was emblematic of a nation in transformation. This was my introduction to the esoteric tradition. The esoteric was romantic and inspirational; it accentuated the values of meaning, purpose, and direction. At the same time, I felt that I had discovered a potent image that stood for America's greatness.

All nations and humans have a special destiny, which, if fulfilled, leads to their enlightenment. How does one discover personal, national, or world destiny? Meditation, reflection, and prayer are more than just a beginning, but there are other means. The destiny of a nation is often embedded in its national coat of arms or great seal. The seal of a nation usually is a deliberate creation, especially if the nation's founders are conscious of the importance of symbols. America's founders were especially adroit at choosing symbols that expressed the philosophy of the new republic.

It is one thing to express something, however, and another to have it heard, understood, and acted on. The Founding Fathers' intentions were signed into law on June 20, 1782. Since that time, the State Department and Congress have kept half of the Great Seal in the dark, at times intentionally.

The obverse of America's Great Seal is dominated by the eagle. The reverse of the seal bears an eye in a triangle over a pyramid and two Latin mottoes. Most people have seen this symbol only on the back of the one dollar bill. Before 1935, when it was placed on currency, very few Americans had ever seen it at all.

It was not until 1891 that the State Department allowed access to its department files on the Great Seal. Because of this, early seal historians and subsequent generations of historians who depended on sources predating 1891 were often misinformed.

In 1976 the State Department published the definitive history of America's Great Seal. The document is a godsend to those who wish to know the seal's history. Like earlier State Department publications, however, it rejects the idea of cutting a die of the seal's reverse.

What the State Department has not considered is the consequences of not recognizing the importance of the founders' vision of America. Will our neglect impair the fulfillment of our national destiny? It seems to me that, by ignoring the vision of our Founding Fathers, we have altered our capacity to fulfill the goals established by those distinguished men. In effect, as interest grows in our national symbol, especially its reverse, the whole country is experiencing a greater capacity to comprehend the spiritual vision of those who brought America into being.

Introduction

You may be tired of hearing that America is at a crossroads in history, but it is true. Our nation, and the world, faces a very bleak period ahead, perhaps as dark as the times at Valley Forge. But unlike General Washington, we have been provided a lamp of wisdom to show the way. That lamp is America's coat of arms, and the illumination it is providing is only at half strength. We can adjust the power of our torch by increasing knowledge about its use and knowing where to shine it. This book will provide you with such knowledge. Your willful use of this knowledge may determine America's success in achieving its goals and attaining its spiritual destiny.

Chapter 1

The Amerindian Influence on the Founders' Vision

T HREE opinions about history have influenced my thinking for two decades. The first two have no authoritative
source, but somehow I have always associated them with my
vision of those two powerful European writers, Voltaire and
Francis Bacon: "History is something that never happened,
written by a man who was not there," and "History is the lie
commonly agreed on." It was America's own Henry Ford who
was once credited with saying "History is bunk!" (He later
denied that he'd said it, but agreed with the sentiment it expressed.) A fourth version of this notion is found in the 1739
edition of *Poor Richard's Almanac,* Ben Franklin's creation:
"Historians relate, not so much what is done, as what they
would have believed."

Bacon and Voltaire were painfully conscious that historical accounts, if they were to survive, must not offend those in
charge. For these writers, history was at best a compromise,
full of codes and cyphers to protect not only the authors but
their messages.

Contemporary views of America's Founding Fathers must
analyze just such deliberately disguised truths. It is very
difficult to understand the founders if we depend only on
what historians say about them. Our founders espoused too
many controversial views that they recognized must be care-
fully phrased. We cannot expect to read the inner truths of

history if we only look at the surface of written accounts. Although there may be more information available today on America's democratic origins, the average person still may not be conscious of our country's unfolding, even after the media coverage of the Constitution's bicentennial. When I say our view of the historical origins and founding of American democratic institutions is distorted and incomplete, I do not say it merely to generate controversy. Consider the discovery and colonization of America. What confidence would you have in a professor who clung to the pronouncement that Columbus discovered America? Not much, especially if you already knew that Leif Ericson, the Vikings, and perhaps even the Phoenicians, Africans, and Jews visited America 1500 years before Columbus arrived.

During my undergraduate days I learned that American democracy came from Europe and that this republic was the child of the Age of Reason, out of which grew the democratic ideal. While Europe dreamed of a utopian type of representative government, America manifested it. The distance from Europe afforded us by the Atlantic Ocean played a key role in our successful development of representative government, but that's just part of the story. The political philosophies of Kant, Montesquieu, Locke, and others influenced the thoughts of the men who established the republic. Until recently, however, one of the most important influences on our Founding Fathers has been unrecognized, in part because it is alien to the way we have come to view the "noble savages" who called America their home long before the white man came.

Within the past few decades a new view of the American Indians has begun to emerge. It now appears certain that a group of six Indian tribes joined to promote peace and human rights—the League of the Iroquois—was a major influence on Ben Franklin and Thomas Jefferson. Franklin and Jefferson borrowed consciously and freely from the democratic methods by which these people had governed themselves for four centuries. Without the league's guidance and advice Franklin and Jefferson would not have achieved their goal so well.

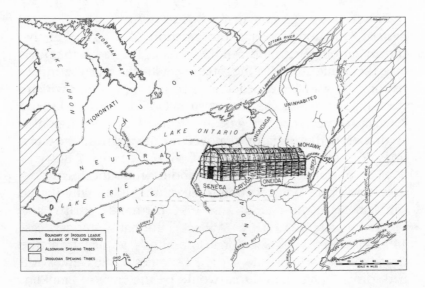

Figure 1:
Map showing the location of the Northern Iroquoian tribes, circa 1600 A.D. (The University of the State of New York, State Museum and Science Service.)

We are born at the right time and place to discover how the American Indian shaped democracy. Dr. Bruce E. Johansen's *Forgotten Founders* (Harvard Common Press, 1982) is a significant contribution to our renewed understanding of how the League of the Iroquois influenced the founding of America. Many share my opinion of Dr. Johansen's research, among them Arthur Schlesinger, Jr., who described the book as "offering justice at last to the Indian contributions to the American Constitution." The book also won high praise from Dee Brown (author of *Bury My Heart at Wounded Knee*). Much of the material in this chapter can be attributed to Dr. Johansen's work.

THE LEAGUE OF THE IROQUOIS

The Indians of the northeast corridor of North America were not always a peaceful race (see Figure 1). In fact, they were perennially at war with one another until, as the Iroquois tradition states, Deganwidah, a Huron from what is now eastern Ontario, proposed the creation of a league of five Indian nations. He found a spokesperson, Hiawatha, to undertake the arduous task of negotiating with the warring Indian nations. Hiawatha succeeded in accomplishing Deganwidah's dream, and the Senecas, Onondagas, Oneidas, Mohawks, and Cayugas ceased their struggle and formed a federal union. A sixth nation, the Tuscaroras, moved northward from the Carolinas, joining the league around 1714.

There is some disagreement about when the league began. Traditional oral accounts suggest A.D. 1000, while some scholars place the date at A.D. 1390 (Arthur C. Parker) and others at A.D 1450 (P.A. Wallace). Probably by at least 1450—forty-two years before Columbus's voyage from the decadent Old World—the so-called savages of the New World had formed a federation that would be the envy of Franklin, Jefferson, and Washington.

Here is what Cadwallader Colden (Johansen, 1982, xiv), a contemporary of Benjamin Franklin, said about the Iroquois:

> [The Indians] have "outdone the Romans" . . . . [They have] a social and political system so old that the immigrant Europeans knew nothing of its origins—a federal union of five (and later six) Indian nations that had put into practice concepts of popular participation and natural rights that the European savants had thus far only theorized. The Iroquoian system, expressed through its constitution "The Great Law of Peace," rested on assumptions foreign to monarchies of Europe: it regarded leaders as servants of the people, rather than their masters, and made provision for their leaders' impeachment for errant behavior. The Iroquois' law and custom upheld freedom of expression in political and religious matters and it forbade the unauthorized entry of homes. It provided for political participation by women and relatively equitable distribution of wealth . . .

Nineteenth- and twentieth-century historians have supported Cadwallader Colden's conclusions. Lewis Henry Morgan (1881), for example, found that the Iroquoian civil policy prevented the concentration of power in the hands of any single individual and inclined rather to the division of power among many equals. The Iroquois prized individual independence and their government was set up so as to preserve that independence. The Iroquois confederation contained the "germ of modern parliament, congress and legislature."

In Arthur C. Parker's account (1968, 11) of the Iroquois Great Law of Peace he notes, "Here, then, we find the right of popular nomination, the right of recall and woman suffrage flourishing in the old America of the Red Man and centuries before it became the clamor of the New America of the white invader. . . ." Hewitt (1918) observed that the Iroquois league significantly departed from tradition in separating military and civil affairs and in tolerating all forms of religion. The unwritten Iroquois constitution—perhaps the world's oldest—also contained almost all the safeguards ever instituted in historic parliaments to protect home affairs from centralized authority (Pound, 1930). This rich Native American democratic tradition was the real source for the new Americans' distinctive political ideals. Thus centuries before Columbus arrived in the New World, democracy was alive and well, just waiting for the Founding Fathers to discover it.

Are you surprised that the Amerindians established a democratic government of their own before the time of the white man? The colonists also borrowed their diet (corn, white potatoes, turkey, squash, avocados, tomatoes, apples), some of their medicine, language, and clothing. Early settlers—and later Americans—owed their very existence to the Indians. As Felix Cohen (1952) asserted, "The real epic of America is the yet unfinished story of the Americanization of the white man."

THE ANGLO–IROQUOIS ALLIANCE AND THE ALBANY PLAN

Benjamin Franklin became aware and made others aware of the accomplishments of the Iroquois league through his work as a printer. Besides his newspaper, the *Pennsylvania Gazette*, which could be found in Philadelphia's most prominent homes, he published the proceedings of Indian treaty councils as early as 1736. One such council was held in 1744 in

Lancaster, Pennsylvania, where representatives from Maryland, Virginia, and Pennsylvania met with the chiefs of the Iroquois league and agreed to an Anglo–Iroquois alliance. Both sides needed this alliance to halt France's determination to dominate the New World. The colonies agreed to control the recurrent problem of Scotch-Irish frontiersmen who were squatting on Indian land without permission, and in return the Indians would side with the English against France.

In the course of this meeting on July 4, 1744, the Indian spokesperson Canassatego, much revered by both Indians and colonists, advised that the colonies unite, just as the Indians had done centuries before. Johansen (1982, 48) provides this intriguing sketch of what could truly be called one of America's native Indian founding fathers:

> Canassatego was praised for his dignity and forcefulness of speech and his uncanny understanding of the whites. At the 1744 treaty council, Canassatego reportedly carried off "all honors in oratory, logical argument, and adroit negotiation," according to Witham Marshe, who observed the treaty council. Marshe wrote afterward that "Ye Indians seem superior to ye commissioners in point of sense and argument." His words were meant for Canassatego. An unusually tall man in the days when the average height was only slightly over five feet, Canassatego was well muscled, especially in the legs and chest, and athletic well past his fiftieth year. His size and booming voice, aided by a commanding presence gave him what later writers would call charisma—conversation stopped when he walked into a room. Outgoing to the point of radiance, Canassatego, by his own admission, drank too much of the white man's rum, and when inebriated was known for being unflatteringly direct in front of people he disliked. Because of his oratory, which was noted for both dignity and power, Canassatego was the elected speaker of the Grand Council at Onondaga during these crucial years.

In 1747, Cadwallader Colden published the second edition of his *History of the Five Indian Nations Depending on the Province of New York in America* and Franklin read it. Franklin began his campaign for federal union soon after. In 1751, he wrote:

I am of the opinion . . . that securing the friendship of the Indians is of the greatest consequence for these colonies . . . the surest means of doing it are to regulate Indian trade, so as to convince them [the Indians] that they may have the best and cheapest goods, and the fairest dealings with the English. . . . The colonists should accept the Iroquois advice to form a union in common defense under a common, federal government. . . . It would be a very strange thing if six nations of ignorant savages should be capable of forming a scheme for such an Union and be able to execute it in such a manner as that it has subsisted ages, and appears indissoluble, and yet a like union should be impracticable for ten or a dozen English colonies. (Kennedy, 1751)

Franklin served as one of the colony's commissioners at a meeting in 1753 with the six nations in Carlisle, Pennsylvania. The Carlisle Treaty, which supported national defense against the French, began Franklin's diplomatic career. A year later the Albany Congress convened to cement the alliance with the Iroquois and to formulate and ratify a plan of uniting the colonies, as Canassatego had proposed ten years earlier.

The similarities are obvious between the Albany plan of union created by Franklin and the League of the Iroquois Nations. Franklin proposed that a president–general appointed by the crown preside over the colonies. Each state would retain its internal sovereignty and constitution so that distrust among states due to wide diversity of opinions and geographical separation could be somewhat neutralized. The Iroquois resolved this difficulty by requiring that all "states" agree on a particular action before putting it into effect. Another similarity was that Franklin's proposed Grand Council and the Iroquois Great Council were both unicameral, unlike the British bicameral system.

Each colony was to have a quantity of representatives based on population and the number of enlisted military personnel, just as the Iroquois allowed for varying numbers for each of its five nations. Even the numbers of delegates allowed by the Iroquois and Franklin were nearly identical: Franklin suggested forty-eight, the Iroquois allowed fifty.

On the issue of military conscription, Franklin took the middle road. While the crown made it involuntary and the Iroquois voluntary, he suggested that the federal government should not be allowed "to impress men in any colonies without the consent of its legislature" (Franklin, 1754). The Albany Plan also regulated Indian trade and prevented colonial settlers from seizing land the Iroquois wanted.

Franklin's leadership in proposing the Albany Plan made him the progenitor of the colonial union and a federalist system of government. He was too far ahead of his time, though, and the Albany Plan died in the state legislature, which pleased the British. It was to resurface two decades later, after the Stamp Act united the colonies and eventually result in the Articles of Confederation.

In 1754, Franklin published this statement at the conclusion of the Albany Congress:

> Brothers, our forefathers rejoiced to hear Canassatego speak. . . . [His words] sunk deep into our hearts. The advice was good. It was kind. They said to one another: "The Six Nations are a wise people, let us hearken to them, and take their counsel; and teach our children to follow it." Our old men have done so. They have frequently taken a single arrow and said, Children, see how easily it is broken. Then they have taken and tied twelve arrows together with a strong string or cord and our strongest men could not break them. See, said they, this is what the Six Nations mean. Divided, a single man may destroy you; United, you are a match for the whole world. We thank the great God that we are all united; that we have a strong confederacy, composed of twelve provinces. . . . These provinces have lighted a great council fire at Philadelphia and sent sixty-five counsellors to speak and act in the name of the whole, and to consult for the common good of the people . . .

Without the example of Native Americans' democratic union and their assistance, our own republic would likely have taken on a different form. Franklin borrowed heavily from the organization and ideals of the Iroquois league in his early proposals for the structure of the new government. All of the founders drew encouragement from the fact that their

Figure 2:
Detail from Wampum belt commemorating George Washington. (*Akwesasne Notes*, Vol. 19, No. 4. Redrawn by Robin Raindrop.)

Figure 3:
Detail from the Thirteen Diamond Belt given to the thirteen United States by the six Iroquois Nations, 1775–1776. (*Akwesasne Notes*, Vol. 19, No. 4. Redrawn by Robin Raindrop.)

league had been strong for some four centuries—twice as long as the current union on North American soil, which only recently celebrated its second century of existence. Unfortunately, the United States the Amerindians helped to bring into being used its strength to obliterate their own people (see Figures 2 and 3).

Chapter 2

The Founding Fathers
and Secret Societies

CONTEMPORARY historians characterize the seventeenth and eighteenth centuries respectively as the Age of Reason and the Enlightenment, but not all of the mental energy of this period was spent trying to "prove everything—or almost everything—in the world moved according to unchangeable and predictable laws." In fact, other underestimated influences on the founders' ideas (besides the Iroquois league) were various forms of mysticism, occultism, and Illuminism, which used the tools of astrology, alchemy, and the Cabala.

In the colonies, watered-down versions of esoteric teachings could be found in publications known as almanacs. Although not of American origin, the almanacs became more popular here than in the Old World. Tens of thousands of these almanacs, published by Nathaniel Ames and Benjamin Franklin, found their way into almost every home where they were consulted perhaps as frequently as the Bible. In fact, Franklin made his fortune through the extremely popular *Poor Richard's Almanac*. Besides the newspapers and the Bible, the almanacs were by and large the colonies' only generally disseminated reading material.

Almanacs contained scientific and quasi-scientific medicine and Newtonian science for the common people, as well as a great deal of astrology, which was of widespread public interest, and other pseudoscience. Almanacs carried yearly predictions of eclipses of the sun and moon as well as the phases of the moon and weather forecasts, essential for the planting of crops.

SECRET SOCIETIES: A DEFINITION

While the general public had almanacs, secret societies enabled men of the upper classes to gain more direct access to esoteric knowledge. According to two major authorities in the esoteric tradition, Dane Rudhyar and Manly Palmer Hall, some of the Founding Fathers were active members of these organizations.

The secret society tradition is an ancient one. Esoteric historian C. Heckethorn (1966) believes that the great secret societies of antiquity were justified in their exclusive practices because the knowledge they guarded was so profound and important that it could not be made available to everyone. Their procedures were to lead the initiate in stages to an understanding of the universal mysteries of life. Contemporary secret societies do not hide their existence; their general activities, with some care and discrimination, can be investigated. Their inner sanctum, however, is still largely unknown.

The inner teachings of most secret societies deal with self-transformation, that is, knowledge and mastery of humanity's physical, emotional, mental, and spiritual powers. Noted theosophical and Masonic authority Charles Leadbeater reveals how the process of self-transformation is woven into the fabric of Freemasonry's three degrees:

> In each of the previous Degrees I have referred to certain currents of etheric force which flow through and around the spine of every human being . . . .
> It is part of the plan of Freemasonry to stimulate the activity of these forces in the human body in order that evolution may be quickened. . . . the first Degree . . . affects the "Ida" or feminine aspect of the force, thus making it easier for the candidate to control passion and emotion; in the Second Degree it is the "Pingala" or masculine aspect which is strengthened in order to facilitate the control of

the mind; but in this Third Degree it is the central energy itself, the "Sushumna" which is aroused, thereby opening the way for the influence of the pure spirit on high. It is by passing up through this channel . . . that a yogi leaves his physical body at will in such a manner that he can retain full consciousness on higher planes, and bring back . . . a clear memory of his experiences. (1963, 260)

Freemasons

Albert Mackey (1966), a Masonic author and historian whose views many contemporary Masonic lodges share, states that the term freemason was used to distinguish the mason from operative (working) masons or stonemasons, who were considered an inferior class of workmen. Freemasons were free in the sense that they were able to travel across national borders and work on any great building. Their secret passwords and rituals allowed a mason to identify himself to his fellows and find employment.

William Brown (1968) acknowledges as many as twelve sources of Freemasonry, from the ancient mysteries to the Crusaders, the Knights Templars, the Roman College of Artificers, the operative masons or traveling masons of the Middle Ages, the Rosicrucians, the British Throne, Oliver Cromwell, James the Pretender, and Christopher Wren. More conservative Masonic historians, such as Mackey (1966), think that Masonry was reborn through the efforts of John Desaguliers and James Anderson, compilers of the celebrated *Book of Constitutions* (Anderson, 1738).

Although twentieth-century Freemasonry expresses itself through philanthropy and charity, some suggest that its real purpose is the eternal search for truth, "the truth about God, and the immorality of the soul! The various degrees represent the different levels through which the human mind passes while moving from ignorance toward knowledge" (Brown, 1968, 17). Others note that the role of the creative/intuitive mind in decision making was central to eighteenth- and nineteenth-century Freemasonry, which directed its members in the service of the Divine Architect (Harman, 1979).

Masonic lodges met (and still meet) at regular intervals to carry out instruction and ceremonies. Many of the ceremonies resemble the rites of ancient religious orders and chivalric brotherhoods. In its early years in America, Masonry developed into two forms: the Lodge, with fixed meeting place, where esteemed members might participate in laying the cornerstones for imposing edifices; and the Military Lodge, which depended less on location and more on the strong bonds of brotherhood within the new armies. George Washington would draw great strength from the Military Lodges. Because Masonic members took great pride in such affiliation, numerous histories of individual lodges were eventually made public. Other reports of rituals and ceremonies came from disaffected members or from those who sought to form their own, more public, societies.

Rosicrucians

A second secret society claims that several of America's founders were Rosicrucians. The Rosicrucian order may have originated in Germany in 1614 with the publication of *The Fama of the Fraternity of the Meritorious Order of the Rosy Cross Addressed to the Learned in General and the Governors of Europe*. This book was purportedly the work of an anonymous group of adepts who wanted to work toward the "moral renewal and perfection" of mankind. The group proposed "that all men of learning throughout the world should join forces for the establishment of a synthesis of science, through which would be discovered the perfect method of all the arts" (Spence, 1968, 340).

Many have speculated on the obscure roots of the Rosicrucian fraternity (Heckethorn, 1966; Regardie, 1971; Waite, N.D.; Wittemans, 1938). The Rosicrucian order A.M.O.R.C. (Ancient and Mystical Order of the Rosy Cross) of San Jose, California, teaches that its founder was the "heretical" Egyptian pharaoh Akhenaton (B.C. 1370–1353), the founder of monotheism (Lewis, 1941). Other contemporary writers attribute its founding to Christian Rosenkreutz, who is supposed to have lived in the sixteenth and seventeenth centuries and who is cited in the *Fama Fraternitatis* (1614) as having learned the "sublime science" of alchemy in the East (Allen, 1968; Heckethorn, 1966).

One of the preeminent nineteenth century Freemasonic scholars of highest degree, Albert Pike, explained the purpose of the Rosicrucians (1906, 289):

> The obligations of our Ancient Brethren of the Rose were to fulfill all the duties of friendship, cheerfulness, charity, peace, liberality, temperance and chastity: and scrupulously to avoid impurity, haughtiness, hatred, anger, and every other kind of vice. They took their philosophy from the old Theology of the Egyptians, as Moses and Solomon had done, and borrowed its hieroglyphics and cyphers of the Hebrews. Their principal rules were, to exercise the profession of medicine charitably and without fee, to advance the cause of virtue, enlarge the sciences, and induce men to live as in the primitive times of the world.

The word *Rosicrucian* is also of uncertain origin. It may have been derived from the name of its alleged founder Christian Rosenkreutz. It may have been composed from the Latin words *ros* (dew) and *crux* (cross); *ros* representing the alchemical dew of the philosophers, the most powerful solvent of gold, and the cross symbolizing light (Spence, 1968, 340).

Only in the last fifteen years have contemporary scholars turned their attention to the origins and meaning of Rosicrucianism. According to Peter French (1972, 14), "The Rosicrucian mode of thinking . . . tended toward secrecy and science mixed with magic." Frances Yates (1972), fellow of the British Academy and the Royal Society of Literature, sees Rosicrucianism in a historical context. For her, it represents a phase in European culture intermediate between the Renaissance and the scientific revolution of the seventeenth century. "It is a phase in which the Renaissance Hermetic–Cabalist tradition has received the influx of another Hermetic tradition, that of alchemy." Yates supports the thesis that the Rosicrucian movement arose from an alliance of Protestant sympathizers that was formed to counteract the Catholic League. European culture was in need of reform—in its society, education, and religion—and the Catholic League opposed and temporarily subdued such reforms until Renaissance science brought into being the scientific revolution. In contrast, the Rosicrucian enlightenment strove not only for the advancement of intellectual knowledge but also for spiritual illumination.

Many authors have noted that Rosicrucians and Freemasons share many symbols and beliefs, but there is disagreement as to which order preceded the other (Mackey, 1966; Waite, N.D. ; Wittemans, 1938). Some writers suggest that the Masonic and Rosicrucian orders cooperated with one another in colonizing the New World. According to the esoteric tradition (Hall, 1951; Perkins, 1971), Sir Francis Bacon was a prime mover of both Rosicrucian and Freemasonic Orders. He heavily lobbied Queen Elizabeth I to colonize the New World to prevent its domination by Spain, and hence by the Catholic League, which (as already noted) opposed the social, economic, and religious reforms proposed by Freemasonry and Rosicrucianism.

Wittemans (1938) describes the difference between the two organizations in this way:

> The Freemasons and the Rosicrucians have become disunited . . . in order to propagate, as to the former, philosophical ideas, philanthropy, religious liberty, cosmopolitanism; as for the latter, in order to continue Kabbalistic, alchemical and magical dreams of their predecessors. In order to keep to the probable, it is necessary to recognize in these illuminati several characteristics: That of guardians of the esoteric tradition; that of interpreters of the light of the Gospels; that of physicians of bodies, souls and societies; finally that of forerunners, or precursors of the Holy Spirit. (p. 93)

Wittemans also suggested that Freemasonry is "exoteric Rosicrucianism," by which he meant that it was a worldly expression of the fundamental ideals of the Rosicrucians.

The Illuminati

A third secret society also has been linked to a few of the Founding Fathers. The name *Illuminati* has been adopted by a number of sects, but the Bavarian Society of the Illuminati, founded by Adam Weishaupt, a professor of law at Ingolstadt University in 1776, is the best known and most connected with several of the founders.

The Bavarian Illuminati was founded on May 1, 1776. This organization (five members at the time of its founding) was sworn to remove all heads of Church and State.

Manly Hall (1950) believed that this Bavarian group and their leader, Adam Weishaupt, served a higher cause, and was but a fragment of a larger movement:

> Weishaupt emerged as a faithful servant of a higher cause; behind him moved the intricate machinery of the secret schools. As usual, they did not trust their full weight to any perishable institution. The physical history of the Bavarian Illuminati extended over a period of only twelve years. It is difficult to understand, therefore, the profound stir which this movement caused in the political life of Europe. We are forced to the realization that this Bavarian group was only a fragment of a large and composite design. (p. 79)

Weishaupt's Illuminati Society was divided into three classes, one of which was named Masonry, and so he succeeded in linking the Illuminati and Masonic orders (Mackey, 1966; Spence, 1968). The Illuminati at its peak had at least 2,000 members, some of them the most distinguished men in Germany, but its popularity was short-lived (Heckethorn, 1966; Mackey, 1966; Spence, 1968). In 1784, the elector of Bavaria issued an edict for its suppression (Mackey, 1966), and by the end of the eighteenth century the Illuminati had ceased to exist (Heckethorn, 1966; Mackey, 1966). Some authors whose philosophy is aligned with that of the John Birch Society believe that it continued to function (Carr, 1970; Robison, 1967; Webster, N.D.).

Some researchers have suggested that the Illuminist conspiracy was responsible for the French Revolution (Robison, 1967; Webster, N.D.). It has been feared that the Illuminati had infiltrated America (through Masonry) at the end of the eighteenth century. These allegations are largely unsubstantiated. Contemporary authors subscribe to the theory that the true Illuminists were political clergy and the Federalist leaders who were making a last effort to discredit the Jefferson administration.

It is important to note that the word "illuminati" also referred to one who was enlightened by receiving knowledge from an exalted or higher source. The term was first used in 1492, but may have had its origin in Gnosticism or in the Mystery Schools of the East. The Rosicrucian order, as well as other esoteric groups, uses the term "illuminati" to refer to the higher grades of initiation. To more conservative historians, the Illuminati "was instituted for the purpose of lessening the evils resulting from the want of information, from tyranny, political and ecclesiastical" (Heckethorn, Vol. 1, 1966, 306).

If we accept Heckethorn's definition of the Illuminati's purpose, then most of our Founding Fathers would have supported its goals, since America was founded on freedom of information and against political and ecclesiastical tyranny.

THE METAPHYSICAL LEANINGS OF THE FOUNDERS

Esoteric historians assert that from nine (Heaton, 1965) to fifty (Hall, 1951) of the nation's founders were Freemasons. The wide discrepancy in these figures is due to records missing or destroyed during the Revolutionary War and to the uneven quality of the remaining evidence of Masonic membership. The best and clearest evidence is the date and lodge of initiation. This type of evidence yields a total of nine members. Less acceptable evidence is the dates of lodge attendance and attendance at Masonic functions.

Four of the nation's founders are alleged to have been Rosicrucians (Washington, Jefferson, Franklin, and Charles Thomson), and three (Franklin, Jefferson, and Adams) are thought to be initiates in the Illuminati order (Carr, 1970). All claims of the Founding Fathers' involvement with the Rosicrucians and Illuminati originated from the organizations themselves and other unverifiable sources (Hieronimus, 1975).[1]

[1.] A lengthy treatment of Freemasons, Rosicrucians, and Illuminati and their reputed influence on George Washington, Benjamin Franklin, and Thomas Jefferson can be found in a two-part article "Were our Founding Fathers Occultists?" (Hieronimus, 1975) and is summarized in *The Two Great Seals of America* (Hieronimus, 1976).

Although it is generally recognized that many of the founders were affiliated with secret societies, this element of their lives is usually ignored or acknowledged only in a derogatory remark. Two examples of such discrediting illustrate this common practice. One of Washington's biographers captioned a painting of Washington presiding over a lodge: "Below: a lithograph by Duval and Hunter showing Washington in a Masonic Lodge. He was a member but not a very active one. Undoubtedly the illustration was used by the order to capitalize on what was only a nominal membership" (Orlandi, 1967, 13). Franklin's involvement with Masonry was downplayed similarly by A.O. Aldridge (1967, 156):

> A few years before the Kinnersley affair, Franklin became a Mason; and subsequently took an active part in both the Philadelphia Lodge and the Parisian Lodge of the Nine Sisters. Since Eighteenth century Masonic doctrine was almost inseparable from deism, there is little purpose in detailing this segment of Franklin's religious history. In his Masonic rites he referred to God as "the Supreme Architect" and to his fellow members as "brothers," but otherwise, Masonic ritual had but little to contribute to his spiritual life.

The authors do not appear to be familiar with the true extent of either Washington's or Franklin's participation in Masonry, nor do they seem to have much knowledge of Masonic beliefs and practices.

George Washington

Mackey's *Revised Encyclopedia of Freemasonry* (1966) clearly shows that Washington's membership in the order was more than token.

> Washington was initiated, in 1752, in the Lodge at Fredericksburg, Virginia, and the records of that Lodge, still in existence, present the following entries on the subject. The first entry is thus: "Nov. 4th. 1752. This evening Mr. George Washington was initiated as an Entered Apprentice," receipt of the entrance fee, amounting to £23s., was acknowledged, F.C. and M.M. March 3 and August 4, 1753.
> On March 3 in the following year, "Mr. George Washington" is recorded as having been passed a Fellow Craft; and on August 4, same year, 1753, the record of the transactions

Figure 4:
White satin Masonic apron embroidered with Masonic emblems
by Marquise Lafayette. Gift from
General Lafayette to George Washington, 1784. (*Holy Bible, Red
Letter Edition, Masonic Edition,*
1960.)

of the evening states that "Mr. George Washington," and
others whose names are mentioned, have been raised to the
Sublime Degree of Master Mason. (pp. 1093–1095)

General Lafayette and General Washington shared not
only a close friendship but membership in the Craft, a commonly used name for Freemasonry. On two occasions General Lafayette presented Masonic aprons to Washington (see
Figure 4). One of these aprons, embroidered in colored silks
by Madame Lafayette, bore the emblems of the Holy Royal
Arch degree. The fact that this apron was especially made for
George Washington has led to much speculation that he was
raised to that degree. This may be of considerable importance,
for the "Royal Arch degree is the salient, spiritual degree of
Freemasonry, not excepting the degree of Master Mason"
(Steinmetz, 1946, 67).

While he was commander in chief of the American armies during the Revolutionary War, Washington frequently attended the meetings of military lodges. He presided over Masonic ceremonies initiating his officers and frequently attended the Communications of the Brethren (lodge meetings). Washington was nominated for Grand Mastership of the Independent Grand Lodge, an office he declined. In 1805, this lodge was renamed Alexandria Washington in his honor.

To Masonic authorities, the evidence is clear that Washington was the master of a lodge. Testimony given by Timothy Bigelow in a eulogy before the Grand Lodge of Massachusetts two months after Washington's death indicates that Washington's Masonic experience was more than perfunctory.

> The information received from our Brethren who had the happiness to be members of the Lodge over which he presided for many years, and of which he died the Master, furnishes abundant proof of his persevering zeal for the prosperity of the Institution. Constant and punctual in his attendance, scrupulous in his observance of the regulations of the Lodge, and solicitous, at all times, to communicate light and instruction, he discharged the duties of the Chair with uncommon dignity and intelligence in all the mysteries of our art.

In his letters and addresses to Masonic bodies, Washington repeated his profound esteem for their principles. In 1797, he addressed the Grand Lodge of Massachusetts: "My attachment to the Society of which we are all members will dispose me always to contribute my best endeavors to promote the honor and prosperity of the Craft" (Sachse, 1915). Later in the same speech he said that the Masonic institution was one whose liberal principles are founded on the immutable laws of truth and justice and whose grand object is to promote the happiness of the human race. Only thirteen months before his death he declared to the Grand Lodge of Maryland, "So far as I am acquainted with the doctrines and principles of Freemasonry, I conceive them to be founded in benevolence, and to be exercised only for the good of mankind. I cannot, therefore, upon this ground, withdraw my approbation from it" (Mackey, 1966, 1095).

Historians have offered many reasons for the fact that a rag-tag American army, led by a general who had to go to the library to brush up on battle tactics, could defeat the strongest military power in the world. Many valid factors have been cited—the barrier of the Atlantic Ocean, the weakness of King George and his problems at home, the guerrilla tactics of the American army, etc.—but what has been overlooked is the influence of secret societies, especially Freemasonry, on America's leaders. Some esoteric historians (Hall, 1951; Case, 1935) cite that of the 56 signers of the Declaration of Independence, at least 50 were Freemasons. Whether this is a fact or not cannot be presently corroborated, but substantial information supports that many of the officers and enlisted men in the American military were Freemasons and many practiced the craft in the military lodges. According to General Lafayette (a Freemason himself), Washington "never willingly gave independent command to officers who were not Freemasons. Nearly all the members of his official family, as well as most other officers who shared his inmost confidence, were his brethren of the mystic tie" (Morse, 1924, ix).

Freemasonry allowed Washington greater control of and influence on his army. Those who breached military and Masonic secrets faced the penalty of death. Manly Hall (1951) and Paul F. Case (1935) report that 12 of Washington's generals were Freemasons, and that this, in part, accounted for their strong allegiance during America's darkest hours.

The underlying philosophy of Freemasonry ("The brotherhood of man and the Fatherhood of God") was the foundation of political, religious, social, and educational reform, which was opposed by the monarchies of Europe and ecclesiastical authorities as well. Washington's leadership and involvement with the craft gave him the confidence that America's military secrets were safe. His involvement in Freemasonry, as Master of the Lodge, provided him with more than confidence, because the lodge ritual's function was to elevate the participant's consciousness.

A group of Freemasons experiencing the rituals and initiations in an altered state of awareness provided the internal strength and fortitude for them to grasp the importance of the

American revolutionary experience, and its meaning for humanity as a whole.

Thus the Atlantic Ocean, guerrilla tactics, and King George's conflicts contributed to the defeat of the English army, but so did the Freemasonic experience. It provided Washington the will and capacity to defeat King George when the world expected America's defeat.

Washington's reputed involvement in the American Rosicrucian Supreme Council is documented in an account entitled, "The Fulfilment of the Prophecy, The Consecration of Washington, The Deliverer, The Wissahickon." The Wissahickon, a creek in Philadelphia, has a special meaning for Rosicrucians.

> Wissahickon is much more than a word, or the name of a stream, however beautiful. To the true American it is synonymous with a pure Mystic religion, with the freedom of all religious sects, for it was here that the many sectarians established themselves; with the founding of the American Republic, because here was conceived the constitution, and here was held the first American Rosicrucian Supreme Council, here was Washington, one of its Acolytes consecrated, and here formed the Grand Temple of the Rosy Cross. Wissahickon the beautiful and to many of us, sacred as the Ganges is to the Hindu. (Clymer and Ricchio, 1972, 59)

Our Story of Atlantis, or the Three Steps, describes the part the mystics of the Wissahickon played in founding America. There can be no doubt that Washington was familiar with and admired several of these mystics and occultists (such as Peter Miller who translated the Declaration of Independence into European languages, and Conrad Beissel), for it was Miller who convinced General Washington not to hang one of America's first traitors but to release him to Miller's custody. Familiarity with Washington's policies toward traitors to the American cause allows one appreciation of the magnitude of Washington's favor. It seems clear that Washington respected Miller and the mystics of the Wissahickon, but the nature of the friendship remains a mystery.

Washington's views on the Illuminati, however, are very clear. He condemned them as "self-created societies" and dealt them a blow that led to their disappearance. When questioned about whether or not Illuminism had spread to Masonry in America, Washington answered that he "did not believe that the lodges of Freemasons in this country had as societies, endeavored to propagate the diabolical tenet of the former [Illuminati] or pernicious principles of the latter [Jacobinism]" (Sparks, 1848, 11: 377).

George Washington's metaphysical leanings are fairly well known; the depth of his spirituality is less so. During the Valley Forge episode his inner strength was perhaps the deciding factor in his ability to hold together what was left of his army (whom he sometimes referred to as his "Christian soldiers"). Washington spent a long time each day in prayer and meditation. This habit of his is well known, and etchings of Washington on his knees beneath the trees of Valley Forge are common. He carried his daily practice of prayer into the lives of his soldiers, ordering prayers to be said in the army every morning, and on Sunday when no chaplain was available he read the Bible to his men and led the prayers himself (Heline, 1949).

Washington's speeches and correspondence held many indications of his spiritual nature. Writing to Governor Trumbull of Connecticut, Washington confesses that he could "almost trace the finger of Divine Providence" through those dark and mysterious days which led the colonists to assemble in convention, thereby laying the foundation for prosperity, when he had "too much reason to fear that misery and confusion were coming too rapidly upon us."

Esoteric tradition recognizes two prophecies related to Washington. One is a possible vision he had at Valley Forge, during which an "angel" showed him America's future. Another account is an alleged Indian prophecy given to Washington by an old chief in 1770. The old sachem reportedly believed that the Great Spirit protected and guided Washington's footsteps through the trials of life, and that Washington would become the chief of many nations of a people yet unborn, hailed as the founder of a mighty empire (Lawrence, 1931).

The astrological chart of George Washington computed for February 22, 1732, 10:15 a.m., also supports Washington's spiritual inclinations and a direct access to his subconscious and unconscious minds, making him prone to unexpected vision and expanded consciousness. At Washington's birth the sun was in the sign of Pisces, which predisposes natives to an intuitive, mystical, religious orientation. These abilities were tempered and structured by his lunar placement in the sign of Capricorn, the sign of structured hierarchical form, which gave Washington organizational stability. The ability to take abstract ideas and structure them into a philosophical system of life is shown by the moon in the ninth house, the house of higher mind and philosophy.

An additional grounding influence is present in Washington's rising sign of Taurus. With Taurus as an ascendant, the president's demeanor would have been slow, thorough, and patient. Yet another force drawing his mystical ideas into form is the moon trining the ascendant.

A mystic is one who has intuitions or intimations of the existence of inner and spiritual worlds, and who attempts to come into self-conscious communion with them. An occultist studies the hidden aspects of being, the science of life or universal nature. It is one who studies the structure and operations as well as the origin and destiny of the cosmos. Mysticism is a product of the heart, while occultism is primarily a product of the mind.

The metaphysical leanings of George Washington were decidedly mystical rather than mental or occult; Washington was heart-centered rather than mind-centered. Benjamin Franklin's metaphysical tendencies, in contrast, were mental and practical.

Benjamin Franklin

Thomas Jefferson referred to Ben Franklin as the greatest ornament of the age and country in which he lived, while others, such as William Pitt, believed that Franklin ranked with Isaac Newton as a scientist. Masonic historians considered this eighteenth-century genius the greatest American Mason of all time. This may surprise those who have read his autobiography, for it makes no mention of this affiliation even though sixty years of his life were involved with the Craft (Sachse, 1906). Little wonder that modern historians have rejected Freemasonry's influence on his spiritual life. Franklin may have chosen to omit his Masonic life from his autobiography because he took his vows of secrecy seriously. (Secrecy has always been of prime importance to Masonry, especially during the revolutionary period.) Because his autobiography was written piecemeal, no complete English edition was available until 1868 (seventy-eight years after Franklin's death), which further complicates the problem of verifying his involvement with the Masons.

The subject of Masonry interested Ben Franklin years before he was qualified to apply for membership at age twenty-one. Since membership in the Craft was largely confined to the gentry, his entrance was delayed until he achieved greater status. His exclusion did not prevent him from publishing articles on Masonic events.

After returning from London in 1726, Franklin founded his own secret society called the Leather Apron Club. The name of the organization itself indicates a Masonic influence, since Masonic aprons were made of leather. The group evolved into the Junto Club in 1731 and eventually became the American Philosophical Society. James Logan, eminent Quaker scholar, denounced it as a political tool of Pennsylvania's Governor Keith. Corinne Heline describes the Leather Apron Club as being small (twelve members) and devoted to preparing members for citizenship in a yet-to-be-born nation. Under the club's auspices, Franklin started the first circulating library and himself became its first librarian.

> The Junto became the center for disseminating the highest idealism cultural and political, into the life of the growing state. In a deeply mystical ceremony, closely resembling the Masonic in form, the members of this club dedicated themselves "to build a universe of peace, devoid of fear and based on love. (1949, 35)

Meanwhile Franklin had attained his heart's desire in being invited to join a Masonic group in Philadelphia in 1730 (see Figure 5). His subsequent Masonic career was highly distinguished (Mackey, 1966, 374), including service as Grand

Figure 5:
Benjamin Franklin adorned in cer-
emonial Freemason apron. (Grand
Lodge of Pennsylvania.)

Master of Pennsylvania and Provincial Grand Master. In 1734, according to Masonic tradition, he and the brethren of Philadelphia's Saint John's Lodge laid the cornerstone of Independence Hall. Twenty years later, he helped to dedicate the first Masonic building in America, Philadelphia's Freemasons' Lodge.

Franklin's participation in lodge activities was serious and steady. Over a period of five years he missed only five lodge meetings and he was never absent from a Grand Lodge meeting (Sachse, 1906, 33). His involvement with Masonry reflected many of the public projects that Masonry was famous for, such as street lighting and cleaning and building hospitals and libraries.

Franklin is supposed to have founded yet another secret society, the Appollonian Society. Heline (1949) notes that at Franklin's time, "Paris was now the center of Egyptian Masonry and occultism flourished everywhere. The [purpose of the] deeply esoteric Appollonian Society . . . was yet again to further his lifelong dream of uniting science with religion. The society celebrated his eighty-third birthday by the erection of his statue crowned with myrtle and laurel."

Benjamin Franklin had occultist tendencies. He was a student of the science of life and nature. Masonry provided some tools for Franklin to plot his and America's course. He printed Masonic by-laws, manuals, and constitutions. Careful examination of his life reveals that the structure and content of his daily life were in harmony with Freemasonic teachings. He practiced morning and evening meditations and reflections on what good he had done for his fellow man that day. The methods by which he sought to improve his moral and ethical character, and his sincere desire to serve the public good through establishing services such as libraries, firehouses, streetlighting, and hospitals, are supported by Freemasonry. His attempt at vegetarianism, concern for life after death, and possible belief in reincarnation could also be interpreted as having Freemasonic influence.

Soon after Franklin arrived in France to negotiate a treaty of alliance (December 4, 1776) he affiliated with the French Masonic lodges. He was present and assisted in the initiation of Voltaire in the Lodge of the Nine Sisters on April 7, 1778. The following year Franklin was elected Worshipful Master of the Nine Sisters' Lodge and served for two years, and again in 1782. Franklin later affiliated with two other French lodges: Saint Jean de Jerusalem (1785) and Loge des Bons Amis (1785).

Franklin used his French and American Masonic connections (especially the Marquis de Lafayette) to cement the Franco-American alliance that contributed immeasurably to America's military success. Diplomacy and secret negotiations are consistent with Masonic protocol, and Ben Franklin was a keen observer and a master practitioner.

Although no hard evidence exists to prove it, at least one Rosicrucian order has claimed Benjamin Franklin as a member. The former Imperator of the Rosicrucian Order, A.M.O.R.C., makes his case this way:

> The truth of the matter is that Franklin did establish a secret group of Rosicrucians that met as a separate body in Philadelphia . . . The one started by Franklin was one of the earliest of the typical, modern forms of lodges that were

communities where the members lived together in a sort of secret community life. (Graves, 1938, 181)

Other sources also imply that Ben Franklin was a Rosicrucian. Heline (1949, 32) mentions a group Franklin led that may have been the Rosicrucian lodge Dr. H. Spencer Lewis refers to in Orval Graves' article "Benjamin Franklin as a Rosicrucian" (1938).

> . . . a mystic brotherhood . . . was located in what is now the Germantown section of Philadelphia . . . upon the passing of its last leader its occult library was turned over to Benjamin Franklin. Naturally, this literature stimulated Franklin's interest in the Ancient Wisdom teachings still further and it was not long before he had gathered around him a group of brilliant youths who were also interested in metaphysical research. Their student occult practices led them far afield and into work more advanced than that pursued by the average twentieth century student of the subject.

The *Rosicrucian Digest* (November 1960, 420) states that Franklin's first connection with the Rosicrucians was a meeting with Conrad Beissel and Michael Wohlfarth of the Ephrata community, during which they discussed publishing their religious material.

It is impossible now to determine the facts of Franklin's Rosicrucian membership, but his involvement may show in his life and accomplishments. It was not until Franklin's return from London in 1726 that his life reflected any order or design. One man may have been responsible for this change, a man who after a four-year relationship with Franklin had become, in Franklin's own words, a second father to him. Very little is known about Mr. Thomas Denham, a Quaker merchant. Mr. Denham paid for Franklin's voyage home from London and offered him a job as a clerk in his store.

The limited information available about Denham indicates that he was a quiet, successful, respected man of sound principles. Many of the conclusions Franklin set down as his own may have stemmed from the observations of the father-like figure he idolized. In my opinion the unsentimental Franklin adopted Denham's ideas without crediting their source. The period following his four years with Denham gave birth to the Leather Apron Club, the Junto, and his entrance into Freemasonry.

Six months after returning to Philadelphia, and shortly after Franklin's twenty-first birthday, both Denham and Franklin became ill. Denham died and Franklin came close to death as well. After recovering, Franklin returned to the printing trade. Franklin's close call with death encouraged him to acquire from an unacknowledged source, or possibly to compose, his own epitaph. This piece of writing suggests that he believed in reincarnation: "The Body of B. Franklin Printer (like the cover of an old book, its contents torn out and stript of its lettering and gilding) lies here, food for worms, but the work shall not be lost; for it will [as he believed] appear once more, in a new and more elegant Edition Revised and corrected by the author."

Prior to Franklin's relationship with Denham, he exhibited at least two other characteristics that might be seen as "Rosicrucian," and perhaps had a third experience suggesting a predisposition to the metaphysical. The first is Franklin's youthful vegetarianism, a practice advised by many secret societies, and one that he believed gave him "greater clearness of head and quicker apprehension" (Franklin, 1967, 27). Second, he made a special pact with a close friend, Charles Osborne. Franklin and Osborne "made a serious agreement that the one who happen'd first to die should, if possible, make a friendly visit to the other, and acquaint him how he found things in that separate state. But he never fulfill'd his promise" (Franklin, 1967, 46). Osborne died first but did not make contact with Franklin after his death. However, their pact was consistent with the Rosicrucian belief in the possibility of communication between the physical and spiritual worlds. Third, Franklin was alleged to have frequented a coffee house that served as a meeting place for "unconventional foreign travelers and soldiers of fortune. Here Franklin discovered a young medical student who was interested in esoteric subjects and so he acquired his intimate companionship. Together they practiced old alchemical formulas, rites and ceremonials" (Heline, 1949, 39).

34

These three facets of his life do not prove Franklin's involvement in the Rosicrucian order nor a predisposition to occultism, but they do show that his life could be interpreted in that light.

After Franklin's initiation into Masonry, he began to publish *Poor Richard's Almanac*. The origin of the almanac's title remains unsettled. Noted Franklin historian Carl Van Doren thinks that "The imaginary astrologer probably took his full name from an actual Englishman, Richard Saunders, compiler of the 'Apollo Anglicus,' though Denham's account lists a Philadelphia Richard Saunders as one of the firm's customers" (Van Doren, 1938, 107). Franklin, being Denham's clerk, was of course familiar with Richard Saunders's name. Is this yet another way Denham influenced Franklin's future plans?

Although he may not have been a serious astrologer, Franklin did use astrology in *Poor Richard's Almanac* to ensure subscribers. It contained an ephemeris, noting the planets' positions, phases of the moon, the changes in season, the length of days, and information on tides. Students of esoteric studies often refer to Franklin's astrological prowess, but there is little evidence to that effect.[2]

Around 1730 Franklin conceived of a plan to achieve moral perfection that consisted of a list of thirteen virtues to master, including frugality, temperance, sincerity, and order. Franklin examined himself mentally every day to determine whether or not he was nearing his desired goal. He then recorded the results in a little book and kept track of his progress. Franklin also held to a strict regimen of scheduling his daily business beginning at 5 a.m. with the question "What good shall I do this day?" and ending at 9 p.m. with the question "What good have I done today?" (Franklin, 1967, pp. 82–85)

An examination of Franklin's ambitious program of scheduling business and moral perfection sheds light on his character. The virtues he prized are basic to the discipline of every true occultist. His scheduling and self-examination of his desire to do good comprise a basic practice of the mystics

---

[2.] For a complete discussion of the Franklin–Leeds astrology episode, see Hieronimus (1975, 1981).

of the Wissahickon (Rosicrucians) and of occultists past and present. Taking the "resolution of the day" and the "examination of the day" can be found in the morning and evening exercises of many meditative groups (Heindel, 1956, 601–606).

Franklin's prediction of important technological advances also points to highly developed psychic and intuitive abilities. In writing to Joseph Priestley he noted:

> The rapid progress true science now makes, occasions my regretting sometimes that I was born too soon. It is possible to imagine the height to which civilization may be carried in a thousand years, as man demonstrates his power over matter. We may, perhaps, learn to deprive larger masses of their gravity and give them absolute levity for the sake of easy transport [the airplane]. Agriculture may halve its labor and double its produce [scientific farming], all diseases may, by sure means, be prevented or cured—not excepting that of old age—and our lives lengthened at pleasure, even beyond the antediluvian standard [preventive medicine]. (Heline, 1949, 38)

Franklin's involvement with the esoteric sciences may be explained by his natal birth chart. According to the astrological chart Marc Penfield erected for Franklin (1972), his sun was in Capricorn in the fourth house. This placement would give him an air of practicality and efficiency, a devotion to home and homeland, and an ability to work with power, in this case as a statesman. With his moon in Pisces in the sixth house, he had a mystical and spiritual bent directed through service. Service is accentuated with his Virgo rising, the sign of the server. Franklin had the analytical mind and facility for communication associated with this Mercury-ruled ascendant: he was a writer and a master printer. He brought great zest as well as philosophical and religious interest to his work for occult and spiritual groups, for whom he printed Bibles. His Mars in Sagittarius in the third house, that of communication, would predispose him to such a combination of interests.

With Uranus in its natural home (the eleventh house) opposing Mercury in Aquarius, Franklin combined the qualities of the intuitive and rational mind. He also showed an interest in matters associated with Aquarian consciousness, such as astrology.

Benjamin Franklin was more than familiar with the esoteric sciences. Whereas George Washington excelled in the areas usually referred to as mystical, Franklin's interests lay more with utilitarian occultism, or the practical occult sciences. This is not to say that Franklin was not visionary in some respects, for he was, but his emphasis was on practicality and mental pursuits rather than the emotional or purely spiritual. Returning from London, Franklin wrote: "The more deeply one studies the inner workings of life, the more wonderful and expansive they become. The more one studies the outer, the less it means and the more ignorant become those who engage in it solely."

When the Constitutional Convention could not reach accord, Franklin made one of his best-known speeches, an appeal for spiritual help in creating the nation.

> . . . God governs in the affairs of men. If a sparrow cannot fall to the ground without His notice, is it probable that an empire can rise without His aid? I . . . believe this and also that without His concurring aid, we shall succeed in this political building no better than the builders of Babel; . . . I therefore beg leave to move—that henceforth prayers imploring the assistance of Heaven and its Blessings on our deliberations be held in this Assembly every morning before we proceed to business. . . . (Cousins, 1958, 18)

Franklin truly was a man ahead of his time, and some of his beliefs and visions were precursors of commonly held views today, such as this one on other life in the universe: "I believe that man is not the most perfect Being but One, rather that as there are many Degrees of Beings his inferiors so there are many Degrees of Beings superior to him" (Aldridge, 1967, 25).

Thomas Jefferson

The third Founding Father considered here strikes a balance between George Washington's heart-centeredness and Benjamin Franklin's mind-centeredness. Jefferson's part in writing the Declaration of Independence, his insistence on the elimination of slavery in America, and his statute on religious freedom in Virginia were essential to America's existence as a new path-breaking nation. Without Jefferson's influence, Alexander Hamilton's views on monarchy might have succeeded, and America would have resembled Europe politically.

Jefferson might have been America's foremost scientist had not his political life interfered. He wrote to Harry Innes, "Science is my passion, politics, my duty." In California today there is a research center named after Jefferson based on Jefferson's behavioristic views and his unique approach to life. In his opinion the most pragmatic and useful sciences were botany, chemistry, zoology, anatomy, surgery, medicine, natural philosophy, agriculture, mathematics, astronomy, geography, politics, commerce, history, ethics, law, and the fine arts. His versatility in studying and writing in all these fields illustrates his special genius.

Because of his scientific attitude, one might be skeptical of his religious interests. In compiling a catalogue for the University of Virginia, which he founded, he refused to assign a special section to metaphysics and incorporated the subject into ethics, saying, "Metaphysics have been incorporated with ethics, and little extension given to them. For while some attention may be usefully bestowed on the operations of thought, prolonged investigations of a faculty unamenable to the test of our senses is an expense of time, too unprofitable to be worthy of indulgence" (Patton, 1906, 265). The eighteenth-century definition of *metaphysics* (literally, after or beyond physics) is not in harmony with the twentieth-century idea that there are laws which are yet undiscovered, but supportive of physical laws, and not in opposition to them. In the recent views of Dr. Willis Harman, president of the Institute of Noetic Sciences, metaphysics (which concerns itself with the ultimate nature of existence) is moving away from a materialistic monism, in which matter gives rise to mind, and toward transcendental monism, in which mind gives rise to matter.

The metaphysical leanings of Jefferson may prove to be the most controversial of the three founders discussed here. Was Thomas Jefferson a member of any secret societies? Masonic sources say he was, but no one has turned up documentary evidence of his initiation. The Masonic *Bible* (1960), however, has "unmistakable evidence that he was an active mason." These include records of his name as a visitor in a

Figure 6:
"Rosicrucian" code found among Jefferson's papers. (Russel M. Arundel, *Everybody's Pixillated*, 1937.)

cornerstone-laying ceremony and references in twenty-nine issues of Masonic journals to his status as a Mason. Jefferson's humanitarian beliefs were harmonious with eighteenth-century Masonry. It has been suggested that Jefferson may have been initiated in France; if so, an American initiation record would not exist.

The Rosicrucians claim Washington and Franklin as members, but do not provide irrefutable evidence. In Jefferson's case, however, Dr. H. Spencer Lewis, former Imperator of the Rosicrucian order, introduces a piece of substantial evidence. Lewis found among Jefferson's papers some "strange-looking characters" that previous researchers had assumed were a code Jefferson had invented (see Figure 6). "I recognized it as one of the old Rosicrucian codes used for many years before Thomas Jefferson became a Rosicrucian, and still to be found in many of the ancient Rosicrucian secret manuscripts" (Heindon, 1961, 126). I have submitted this code to several cryptographers and none have yet been successful in identifying it. Mr. Rex Daniels of Concord, Massachusetts, commented (March 14, 1974), "I have taken several tries at the code with no success for the standard ones. . . . you have hit upon something nobody else seems to know about."

Jefferson's interest in codes and ciphers earned him the title of Father of American Cryptography. His wheel cipher, invented in the late 1700s and still in active use today, "seems to have come out of the blue rather than as a result of mature reflection upon cryptology" (Kahn, 1967, 192–194).

There also exist claims that Jefferson was an astrologer, although my research has yet to substantiate them.

Over the years there have been implications that Jefferson was a member of the Illuminati (Stauffer, 1918, 253). Jefferson's own published criticism of Illuminism, although based on an imperfect acquaintance with the doctrine, seems sincere and balanced. Concerning the work of Adam Weishaupt (founder of the Bavarian Society of Illuminati) and his critics, Jefferson concludes:

> I have lately by accident got sight of a single volume (the 3d.) of the Abbé Barruel's 'Antisocial Conspiracy', which gives me the first idea I have ever had of what is meant by the Illuminatism against which 'Illuminate Morse', as he is now called, and his ecclesiastical and monarchical associates have been making such a hue and cry. Barruel's own parts of the book are perfectly the ravings of a Bedlamite. But he quotes largely from Wishaupt [sic] whom he considers the founder of what he calls the order . . . Wishaupt seems to be an enthusiastic philanthropist. He is among those (as you know the excellent Price and Priestley also are) who believe in the infinite perfectibility of man. He thinks he may in time be rendered so perfect that he will be able to govern himself in every circumstance, so as to injure none, to do all the good he can, to leave government no occasion to exercise their powers over him, and, of course, to render political government useless. This, you know, is Godwin's doctrine, and this is what Robison, Barruel, and Morse have called a conspiracy against all government. . . .
>
> The means he proposes to effect this improvement of human nature are 'to enlighten men, to correct their morals and inspire them with benevolence'. As Wishaupt lived under the tyranny of a despot and priests, he knew that caution was necessary even in spreading information, and the principles of pure morality. He proposed, therefore, to lead the Free Masons to adopt this object. . . . This has given an air of mystery to his views, was the foundation of

his banishment, the subversion of the Masonic Order, and is the color for the ravings against him of Robison, Barruel, and Morse, whose real fears are that the craft would be endangered by the spreading of information, reason, and natural morality among men. . . . I believe you will think with me that if Wishaupt had written here, where no secrecy is necessary in our endeavors to render men wise and virtuous, he would not have thought of any secret machinery for that purpose. . . . (Stauffer, 1918, 312)

Jefferson was forever under attack because of his refusal to attend the church of the presidents. He was slandered as being an atheist during his political campaign, and the Federalists took advantage of this slur. Jefferson's true religious beliefs were Christian in the broadest and truest sense of the word. For years Jefferson worked on compiling a volume he called *The Life and Morals of Jesus of Nazareth*, now known as the *Jefferson Bible* and more fully discussed in my 1975 and 1985 publications. He confided in few people about his studies, but in 1816 Jefferson wrote to Charles Thomson.

I too, have made a wee little book . . . which I call the philosophy of Jesus; it is a paradigma of his doctrines. . . . A more beautiful or precious morsel of ethics I have never seen; it is a document in proof that I am a real Christian, that is to say, a disciple of the doctrines of Jesus. (Jefferson, 1942, x)

Both Jefferson and Franklin had a profound respect for Jesus. Both men were considered deists (some went so far as to say they were atheists), and yet they emphasized a utilitarian religion rather than passive dogma. Jefferson and Franklin exemplified a religion of service for the brotherhood of man (Hieronimus, 1975, 1985b).

One might conclude from Jefferson's rejection of metaphysics that he had no place for visionary experiences, but this is not the case. He, like Franklin and Washington, believed America to have a part in a divine plan. In Jefferson's first inaugural address, he noted that the United States was

. . . kindly separated by nature and a wide ocean from the exterminating havoc of one quarter of the globe; too high minded to endure the degradations of the others; possessing a chosen country, with room enough for our descendants to the hundreth and thousandth generation; entertaining a due sense of our equal right to the use of our own faculties, to the aquisitions of our industry, to honor and confidence from our fellow citizens, resulting not from birth but from our actions and their sense of them; enlightened by a benign religion, professed, indeed, and practiced in various forms, yet all of them including honesty, truth, temperance, gratitude, and the love of man; acknowledging and adoring an overruling Providence, which by all its dispensations proves that it delights in the happiness of man here and his greater happiness hereafter. . . . (Boorstin, 1963, 231)

Jefferson's visions of America can be translated as expansionist. His Louisiana Purchase was not only a landmark in the development of the American nation but an expression of an "Empire for Liberty" that would manifest in the annexing of Canada and Cuba. From this vantage the Monroe Doctrine, which Jefferson strongly urged upon President James Monroe, was not as much a separation of America from Europe as a natural expansion of America's destiny to include the South American continent. In Jefferson's words:

America, North and South, has a set of interests distinct from those of Europe. . . . while the last is laboring to become the domicile of depostism, our endeavor should surely be, to make our hemisphere that of freedom. What a colossus shall we be when the southern continent comes up to our mark! What a stand will it secure as a ralliance for the reason and freedom of the globe! (Boorstin, 1963, 232)

Jefferson's most prized accomplishment, founding the University of Virginia, was based on the traditions of the schools of Athens and Florence and the Alexandrian Library: he wanted to ensure freedom from all theological restraint. Jennings C. Wise theorized that within Jefferson's architectural design of the university are hidden the teachings of the mystery schools and secret societies. Realizing that curricula could be altered, Wise suggests, Jefferson embedded the philosophy of the mystical tradition in the bricks and mortar of the university, so that its design would convey a philosophy free from dogma and superstition. Jefferson unites the ancient architectural elements of the rotunda and the rectangular academic hall, which symbolize heaven (the rotunda as used in the Chaldean Planet Tower called the House of the Seven Spheres) and earth (the four-cornered rectangle). Their use together in one structure symbolizes the union of heaven and earth. A thorough analysis of Jefferson's architectural plans of the University of Virginia, his travels in Europe, and his exposure to ancient architecture is needed to assess Mr. Wise's hypothesis.

An analysis of Jefferson's astrological chart (born April 13, 1743) reveals that his sun is in Aries. The job of the Arian is to align himself with the divine will. The ability to manifest will on the physical plane is shown by the sun in the second house, the house of the material plane. The sun's trine to the planet Mars gives an abundance of energy in the physical world. One of the better aspects is the sun trine to Saturn, which gives him the ability to work slowly, through partnerships, and with those in positions of power and authority. An interesting balance is shown by his sun in square aspect to Uranus, which relates to sporadic revolutionary activity.

Jefferson's sun square with Uranus also shows self-reliance instead of dependence on divine will. Jefferson may have sought a balance between his self and the divine will, between working with those in authority who saw the benefits of his revolutionary ideas and his desire to act immediately regardless of the long-range consequences.

Jefferson's Aquarius rising (symbolizing altruism and brotherhood) indicates that his ultimate motives were geared toward the good of all humankind. Of the three Founding Fathers examined herein, he is the most mysterious. He may have been a member of all three secret societies or perhaps none. He may have had the most profound involvement in the occult sciences, or he may have had few occult leanings.

Jefferson's love of science and love of humanity were equal; he believed that science should be used only for the good of all humankind. This is the promise of the Aquarian age just as it was the promise of Thomas Jefferson.

William Barton and Charles Thomson

What is mysterious in Jefferson's case is clear-cut in the case of the two men directly responsible for the Great Seal's design. There is no certain evidence that either man belonged to an esoteric fraternity. Nor was Pierre Du Simitière, a contributor of several key elements of the seal's design, a member of these organizations. Only Francis Hopkinson, another contributor, was alleged to have been a Freemason.

William Barton (1754–1817) was a native Philadelphian and the son of Reverend Thomas Barton. The younger Barton has sometimes been confused with a Rhode Islander with the same name who was a Mason. He completed his education in Europe and returned to America in 1779. The recipient of two honorary Master of Arts Degrees, he was an accomplished scholar and writer, one work being an essay on the nature and use of paper credit. Barton also wrote on the proper use of coats of arms in the United States.

Charles Thomson, the first Secretary of Congress, was responsible for coordinating the final design of the Great Seal. He befriended and associated with Peter Miller, the mystic who translated the Declaration of Independence into several European languages and thus made Europe aware of America's independence. As a major contribution, Thomson completed the first translation of the Greek Septuagint Bible into Latin. Thomson was adopted into a Delaware Indian tribe in recognition of his fairness and integrity and given an Indian name meaning "Man who tells the truth." He was a close friend of Jefferson and Franklin, the latter of whom was largely responsible for Thomson's political fortunes. Thomson remained firm in his opposition to British policies, actively espousing a radical course from the Stamp Act crisis through the adoption of the Declaration of Independence.

Conclusion

Many authors and students of the esoteric tradition teach and accept the probability that the secret societies had a direct hand in the design of America's seal. A careful analysis doesn't confirm the "obvious." Washington and Franklin were undoubtedly Freemasons and perhaps Rosicrucians. Jefferson cannot be proven a member of any secret society, but future research could change that. Jefferson and Franklin were appointed by Washington to serve on the first committee to design America's seal. Their suggestions were not accepted. They did, however, approve of the seal's final design.

It is the symbols on the seal's reverse that strongly implicate the secret societies' influence. Being Freemasons, Franklin and Washington and perhaps Jefferson approved our two-sided seal because they were capable of interpreting its symbols, which detailed America's secret destiny. An examination of the seal's history and symbols could reveal why so many insist that half of our national seal has occult heritage.

Chapter 3

The History of America's Great Seal

A SIDE from their specific revolt against King George, the colonists' rejection of monarchy as an acceptable system of government was a major step in the evolution of governmental forms. A republic or democracy had been untried since the Athens of the fourth century B.C., even though the British Parliament was, to a limited degree, a representative form of government. America's elected government was a rejection of its origins and a break with its parent, Great Britain, that meant a loss of collective and individual security. Early American history supports the suggestion that the mood of our new nation was one of chaos, confusion, and alienation. It became the task of our fledgling nation to establish a symbol that embodied America's identity. The traditional form of expressing the individuality of a nation is its coat of arms or seal. A seal identifies, authenticates, and documents. Seals predate 4,000 B.C.; the oldest of them have been found in India, Egypt, and what used to be Babylonia and Assyria. To a largely illiterate population, seals served as signatures. Sealing declined after the fall of the Western Roman Empire in 476, but it was revived under Pepin the Short during the eighth century.

Between the eleventh and thirteenth centuries the use of seals spread from sovereigns, high clergy, and nobles to craftspeople and tradespeople. The late twelfth century marked the beginning of the great period of seal engraving that culminated in the thirteenth and fourteenth centuries.

THE GREAT SEAL OF THE UNITED STATES

Great seals originated in the seventh century with European royalty. The first English royal pendant seal, that of Edward the Confessor (who ruled between A.D. 1042 and 1066), became the model for all future British and American seals. The term "great seal" may have emerged during the thirteenth-century reign of King John to differentiate between it and a "privy" or lesser seal, which was used by the sovereign in business and personal matters. The United States adopted the British tradition of using a great seal to authenticate the presidential signature on specific state documents even though it used no lesser seal.

America's Great Seal is its national coat of arms, and it symbolizes the United States government. At one time, it was referred to as the Great Seal of the United States, but since 1892 the State Department has referred to it as the seal of the United States.

Pendant seals, such as America's, are two-sided. During the years of their greatest use, their obverse (front) and reverse (back) were impressed onto two sides of a wax pendant that served to secure ribbons or cords placed between front and back. Being difficult to affix properly and therefore being costly, pendant seals fell into disuse after 1871.

The First Committee

On July 4, 1776, Benjamin Franklin, Thomas Jefferson, and John Adams were given the task of designing the American seal. Pierre Eugene Du Simitière, a portrait painter with some knowledge of heraldry, acted as a consultant and artist to the first committee. Patterson and Dougall (1976, 22) credit Du Simitière with introducing the shield, *E Pluribus Unum*, MDCCLXXVI, and the eye of providence in a triangle.

Esoteric historians frequently exaggerate the contributions and influence of Franklin, Jefferson, and Adams on the seal's accepted design. Each man's suggestions, however, re-

Figure 7:
1856 rendering of the obverse (left) and reverse (right) of the first committee proposal, 1776.

veal how he viewed America's birth and destiny. Franklin's design included (see Figure 7):

> Moses . . . standing on the shore, and extending his hand over the Sea, thereby causing the same to overwhelm Pharaoh who is sitting in an open Chariot, a crown on his Head and a . . . Sword in his Hand. Rays from a Pillar of Fire in the Clouds . . . reaching to Moses . . . to express that he acts by . . . Command of the Deity . . . Motto, Rebellion to Tyrants is Obedience to God. (Patterson and Dougall, 1976, 14)

Jefferson submitted ideas for two sides of the seal. For the obverse, he suggested the children of Israel in the wilderness led by a cloud by day and a pillar of fire by night; on the reverse, he suggested Hengist and Horsa, two brothers who were the legendary leaders of the first Anglo-Saxon settlers in Britain.

Jefferson's and Franklin's suggestions were notably similar in their use of biblical and mythological themes instead of heraldic elements. This could have been due either to their rejection of the Old World philosophy behind heraldry or simply to their ignorance of heraldic design.

John Adams turned to Greek mythology for inspiration (see Figure 8). He proposed an engraving of Hercules resting

Paulo de Matthæis Pinx.   *Sim. Gribelin sculps.*

Figure 8:
For the seal's obverse, John Adams proposed Gribelin's engraving of
Hercules resting on his club. (Patterson and Dougall, *The Eagle and
the Shield*, 1976.)

on his club for the seal's obverse. The moralistic Adams was
perhaps enamored of the choice facing Hercules, on one side
of whom stands Virtue, exhorting him toward a rocky mountain ascent, and on the other, Sloth, voluptuously enticing
him—and presumably the United States as well—down the
less arduous path of pleasure.

Du Simitière's design for the seal's obverse (see Figure 9)
was a shield divided into six sections that represented England, Scotland, Ireland, Holland, France, and Germany. Supporting the shield was the goddess of liberty in a corselet of
armor, a spear and cap in her right hand, her left hand resting
on an anchor symbolizing hope. On the other side, the shield
was held up by a typical American soldier of the day dressed

Figure 9:
Du Simitière's design for the shield's obverse, divided into six sections to represent England, Scotland, Ireland, Holland, France, and Germany. (Patterson and Dougall, *The Eagle and the Shield,* 1976.)

in a hunting shirt of buckskin and equipped with a powder horn and a tomahawk.

The Second Committee

In January 1777, Congress rejected the suggestions of the first committee. A second committee, formed three years later, consulted with Francis Hopkinson, who had successfully designed the American flag, some currency, and numerous official seals for the Board of Admiralty and the Department of the Treasury. Hopkinson's ideas dominated the second committee's report. He proposed white and red stripes within a blue background for the shield, a radiant constellation of thirteen stars, and an olive branch (see Figure 10). Hopkinson's most significant contribution was indirect. For his design of a 1778 50-dollar colonial note, he used an unfinished pyramid device (see Figure 11). This device would reappear later in the proposals submitted by William Barton.

Figure 10:
Hopkinson's drawings of his revised proposals for the obverse (left)
and reverse (right), submitted to the second committee in 1780. (Patterson and Dougall, *The Eagle and the Shield,* 1976.)

Figure 11:
The unfinished pyramid first appeared in Hopkinson's design of a
1778 fifty-dollar colonial note. (Patterson and Dougall, *The Eagle
and the Shield,* 1976.)

Figure 12:
Charles Thomson's drawing for
the third committee, 1782, included an eagle and an unfinished
pyramid for the seal's reverse.
(Patterson and Dougall, *The Eagle
and the Shield,* 1976.)

The Third Committee

The third committee was formed on May 4, 1782, when Secretary of Congress Charles Thomson appointed William Barton
to serve as artist and consultant. His suggestions included an
eagle and an unfinished pyramid for the seal's reverse (see
Figure 12). Thomson placed the eagle in its dominant position
on the seal's obverse. Barton and Thomson borrowed from
the designs of the earlier committees and modified each
other's designs. Their report was submitted and approved on
June 20, 1782 (see Figure 13). Their "Remarks and Explanations" are the only official explanations of the Great Seal's
meaning:

> The Escutcheon is composed of the chief & pale, the two
> most honorable ordinaries. The Pieces, paly, represent the
> several states all joined in one solid compact entire, support-
> ing a Chief, which unites the whole & represents Congress.
> The Motto alludes to this union. The pales in the arms are
> kept closely united by the Chief and the Chief depends on
> that union & strength resulting from it for its support, to
> denote the Confederacy of the United States of America &
> the preservation of their union through Congress.

Figure 13:
Barton and Thomson borrowed
from designs of earlier committees to arrive at this proposal for
the reverse. (Patterson and Dougall, *The Eagle and the Shield*,
1976.)

The colours of the pales are those used in the flag of the
United States of America; white signifies purity and innocence, Red, hardiness and valour, and Blue, the colour of
the Chief signifies vigilance perseverance and justice. The
Olive branch and arrows denote the power of peace & war
which is exclusively invested in Congress. The Constellation denotes a new State taking its place and rank among
other sovereign powers. The Escutcheon is born on the
breast of an American Eagle without any other supporters
to denote that the United States of America ought to rely on
their own virtue.

Reverse. The pyramid signifies Strength and Duration:
The Eye over it & the Motto allude to the many signal interpositions of providence in favor of the American cause. The
date underneath is that of the Declaration of Independence
and the words under it signify the beginning of the new
American Era, which commences from that date (see Figure
14). (Patterson and Dougall, 1976, 84–85)

Figure 14:
The Great Seal today: obverse (left) and reverse (right). The colors are those of the U.S. flag: white signifies purity and innocence; red, hardiness and valor; and the blue color of the chief signifies vigilance, perseverance, and justice. (Patterson and Dougall, *The Eagle and the Shield,* 1976.)

Figure 15:
Impressions of dies cut for the Great Seal in 1782, 1841, and 1885. (Patterson and Dougall, *The Eagle and the Shield,* 1976.)

The first die of the Great Seal was cut from brass in 1782. Subsequently, new dies were cut as the previous ones became worn—in 1825, 1841, 1877, 1885, and 1902—but each time the reverse went uncut and unused (see Figure 15).

Figure 16:
The first official use of the seal's reverse, this commemorative medal was minted in 1882. (Patterson and Dougall, *The Eagle and the Shield,* 1976.)

THE RE-EMERGENCE OF THE NEGLECTED REVERSE

Until 1877 the State Department escaped controversy about its neglect of the seal's reverse. It was then that John D. Champlin, Jr., fired the opening gun on the department. He termed the government's failure to use the reverse after it had been created by law "technically illegal." Champlin's article (1877) aroused public awareness, and in 1882, army officer Charles A.L. Totten requested that a commemoration of the seal showing both sides be struck for the seal's centennial. The commemorative medal was the first official use of the seal's reverse, and it followed the 1786 design (see Figure 16).

On July 7, 1884, Congress appropriated the funds to obtain dies of both sides of the seal. State Department official Theodore Dwight consulted with historical scholars Justin Winsor and Harvard Professor Eliot Norton; genealogist William H. Whitmore, the author of the only American work on heraldry; John D. Champlin, Jr.; and James H. Whitehouse, chief designer of Tiffany and Company, New York. These artists, heraldists, and historians—with the possible exception of Champlin—recommended against reproducing the seal's reverse, largely on esthetic grounds. Norton wrote that the

56

reverse was "practically incapable of effective treatment; it can hardly, (however artistically treated by the designer,) look otherwise than as a dull emblem of a Masonic fraternity" (Patterson and Dougall, 1976, 256).

Hunt (1909) summarizes Dwight's decision this way: "It has undoubtedly been the intention of the Department, when the appropriation was asked for, to cut the reverse; but its purpose was changed after fuller consideration, and it felt at liberty to leave this part of the new law unexecuted, as the law of 1782 remained in part unexecuted for one hundred years."

Patterson and Dougall (1976) feel that the neglect of the reverse was not unlawful. They conjecture that Secretary of State Frelinghuysen had been "misled . . . into thinking that the resolution of the Continental Congress of June 2, 1782, required or ordered the cutting of a die of the reverse, whereas that resolution had simply made available a design for the reverse, to be used if desired to impress the back surface of pendant seals" (p. 245).

As late as 1957 a State Department publication suggested that a die for the reverse may in fact have been cut. In 1973, the author was told by Edwin S. Costrell, the Chief of Historical Studies Division of the State Department, that such a die was never cut.

This scenario was repeated a few years later in a different situation. In 1892 the State Department prepared an exhibit for the Chicago Exposition consisting of two large emblazonments of the seal's obverse and reverse. "The appearance presented by the reverse was so spiritless, prosaic, heavy, and inappropriate that it was never hung" (Hunt, 1909, 61).

THE DOLLAR BILL

The first few decades of the twentieth century saw a growing interest in the seal's reverse. Some esoteric writers predicted that the reverse would soon receive fuller recognition.

In 1934, Secretary of Agriculture and former vice-president Henry A. Wallace submitted a proposal to the president to mint a coin depicting the seal's obverse and reverse. Wallace's interest in the seal's reverse was aroused in 1933 or 1934, when he discovered Hunt's (1909) volume of the seal's history. The Latin phrase *Novus Ordo Seclorum* (new order of the ages) struck him as meaning "the New Deal of the ages." Roosevelt was so impressed with this connection that he decided to place it on the dollar bill, rather than on a coin. Roosevelt's action brought one hundred fifty-three years of obscurity to an end, and the seal's reverse was officially recognized.

Wallace was interested in esoteric topics and was a friend of the Russian mystic Nicholas Roerich. One theory holds that Wallace undertook the promotion of the seal's reverse for cabalistic reasons and that Roerich was Wallace's guru.

There were some basic similarities between Wallace and Roerich. Both were committed to world Federalism; they both opposed the mechanization process, which they thought would threaten individuality; they supported cooperation rather than competition; and they felt that the arrival of a new age was imminent. During this new age humanity would witness the second coming of Christ.

Henry Wallace's daughter, Leslie Douglas (1973, 1974), has rejected the theory that her father was a devotee of Roerich; indeed, she claimed to possess evidence "quite to the contrary." Earl Rogers, librarian at the University of Iowa, the repository of Wallace's papers, notes that Wallace broke with Roerich in 1935. After that he refused to have further contact with Roerich or any member of his family. Schlesinger (1958) agrees with Rogers on this point.

Wallace and Roosevelt were both Masons and so recognized the eye in the triangle as a Masonic emblem. This fact at least confirms that both individuals had been exposed to the symbol and suggests that they may have had personal motives for its popularization.

SOME POSSIBLE REASONS FOR SUPPRESSION OF THE REVERSE

As the currency became available, discussion among scholars opened up. Paul Foster Case took issue with Professor Norton's criticism of the seal's reverse as a "dull emblem of a Masonic fraternity": "A Masonic emblem the design for the reverse of the seal surely is, but he must be ignorant of what it means who calls it dull. It may lack aesthetic appeal, and want finish as a work of art; but as a symbolic statement of the essentials of true Americanism it is a marvel of ingenuity."

But not everyone felt that the reverse's mysterious symbols, assumed to originate from secret societies open only to select white men of the upper classes, expressed the essential spirit of America. Manly Hall, the founder of the Philosophical Research Society in Los Angeles, has stated that ". . . the reverse was not cut at that time because it was regarded as a symbol of a secret society and not the proper device for a sovereign State" (Hall, 1972, 180).

The symbols on the seal's reverse have been used by various secret societies in their ritual regalia and in their lodges of initiation. This does not in itself prove that the seal's reverse is an emblem of any such society but provides us a better understanding of why esoteric historians have linked it with secret societies, and perhaps why those who oppose secret orders would be inclined to reject it.

Many authors in the esoteric tradition have attempted to read into the seal's design meanings that originated with the Freemasons, Rosicrucians, and Illuminati. Many have even claimed it as their own. Carr states that Weishaupt adopted the seal's reverse as the symbol of his new society when he founded the order of the Illuminati on May 1, 1776 (Carr, 1970, xiii). Wyckoff (p. 56), a prominent instructor in the esoteric tradition, taught that "Our beautiful seal is an expression of Freemasonry, an expression of occult ideals."

Although secret societies of the late eighteenth century used the symbols on the seal's reverse, the same symbols were available in books and periodicals found in the colonies. But since none of the four contributors to the seal's design (Thomson, Barton, Pierre Du Simitière, and Frances Hopkinson) were proven members of Masonic or Rosicrucian orders, they were probably influenced by the available literature of their day.

The most frequent error esotericists have made is to assume that the reverse seal's elements are a direct connection to secret societies. They feel that, because at least one and maybe two of the first committee's participants (Jefferson and Franklin) were Freemasons, the reverse seal was a device by which esoteric orders influenced our nation's direction. They contend that the reverse seal in itself is a link to present-day Freemasonry. They ignore the fact that neither Jefferson's nor Franklin's ideas were adopted, except for Jefferson's suggestion of a two-sided seal. This recurring misconception has created pseudohistory in which the seal's factual history and "mythological" or symbolic meanings have become intermingled.

Nevertheless, the popular interest that has surfaced since the seal's appearance on the dollar bill has often focused on the apparent occult significance of the eye in the triangle, pyramid, and mysterious mottoes. In the 1960s, the seal's reverse became an emblem of the counterculture, appearing on posters for dance concerts and in underground newspapers, periodicals, and comic books. In August 1970, the image reentered the general culture consciousness on the cover of *Harper's* magazine. It penetrated scholarly circles in 1974 through its use as a cover device for the *American Quarterly*. Eugene McCarthy employed it in his unsuccessful 1976 bid for the presidency, and even President Ford used it as a theme for a bicentennial speech. The seal's reverse gained an international profile when President Anwar al-Sadat spoke of it as a link between ancient Egypt and modern America (September 1981).

Popular awareness of the symbols on the seal's reverse has continued into the 1980s. Peter Sellers employed the distinctive pyramid and eye motif as a tomb in his final film *Being There*. Shirley MacLaine referred to it in her 1984 book *Out on a Limb* when she described our Founding Fathers as transcendentalists. The character played by Madonna had it embroidered on the back of her jacket in the film *Desperately Seeking Susan*, in which it became an important recurring image.

This public interest may show that Americans are finally ready to accept the images the Founding Fathers chose to represent the new nation. Many esotericists have thought that the reverse's unpopularity meant the time was never right for the populace to discern its meaning. Corinne Heline (1941), for example, believed that: "Altogether its significance is such that it could not be apprehended properly until certain lessons had been learned and realizations acquired such as can come only with approaching maturity. . . . There has not been the consciousness with which to receive it. . . . " Robert Krajenke, a writer on metaphysical subjects, sees this national maturing process in spiritual terms. He has concluded that ". . . only when there is sufficient understanding of spiritual principles throughout the populace will this emblem ever enjoy wide currency and appreciation" (1976b, 43).

Chapter 4

The New Age and
the Great Seal

WESTERN culture is experiencing a transitional period which some call a New Age. Although there are many positive aspects to this new era, it is also viewed, with concern, as a period of historical discontinuity, a crossroads for the human race. Some people think that western culture is disintegrating and that we are nearing a climax in human cultural evolution. They call attention to apocalyptic images of universal destruction and compare our era to the decline of the Roman Empire.

THE SEAL'S REVERSE AS SYMBOL
OF A NEW PARADIGM

The renewal of interest in the seal's reverse suggests an alteration in American values. A gradual identification with the values represented by the seal's reverse and a shifting away from the seal's obverse might reflect the current theory that American culture is undergoing a paradigm shift.

A paradigm is a theoretical pattern or a collective framework of thought (Kuhn, 1970). A new paradigm does not necessarily represent more knowledge than the old one but rather a new perspective. When a critical number of people accept a new idea, a collective paradigm shift occurs.

63

Marilyn Ferguson believes that we are the "children of transition" (1980, 51) and are not fully conscious of the new powers of mind that have been unleashed. She theorizes that we are emerging from an old into a new world paradigm in terms of power, politics, economics, medicine, and education. The old paradigm is characterized by centralization, conquest, rationality, and exploitation. It is symptom, product, and performance oriented, separating body and mind by using the analytic and linear ("left hemisphere") brain functions. The analytic mind controls speech; it adds, subtracts, measures, compartmentalizes, organizes, names, pigeonholes data, and watches clocks. Linear thinking fits information into patterns and categorizes experience.

The old paradigm focused on capitalism, science, and industry. Under its force, economic rationalism developed, a trend that supported society's move away from religion and the tendency to organize activities rationally in utilitarian patterns. Management, optimized efficiency, and economic values became a pseudoethic shaping society's choices.

The new paradigm is described as less stable but more flexible and decentralized, with an emphasis on partnership, conservation, and cooperation. It is rational, intuitive, and process oriented. Its medicine is cause oriented and holistic.

So-called right hemisphere thinking (intuitive reasoning) responds to novelty and the unknown. It is more musical and sexual than the other hemisphere and thinks in images, sees in wholes, and detects patterns. A key characteristic of the new paradigm is transformation.

The new paradigm grows out of the awareness that unlimited technological and economic growth and energy consumption will eventually have to end. The concept of unlimited growth is so deeply embedded in the fundamental assumptions of the old paradigm that it may only be answered if society evolves toward a new guiding paradigm. Harman (1977) suggests two guiding ethics to replace the fragmented materialistic ethics. The ecological ethic fosters a sense of total community of humankind, of human responsibility for the fate of the planet. It connects self-interest to the interests of all present and future generations. The self-realization ethic holds that the proper end of all individual experience is the evolution of the human species and that the appropriate function of social institutions is to create environments that foster this evolution. Harman believes that the ecological and self-realization ethics are complementary, not contradictory. Each allows for cooperation, wholesome competition, love, and individuality.

This change in our cultural paradigm may mirror a change in American cultural symbolism. Hence the renewed interest in the seal's reverse. The fundamental structure of the seal's obverse may be seen as representative of the old paradigm: its elements radiate from a central shield, and the eagle symbolizes the conqueror, competitor, and exploiter. The symbols and their arrangement project centralization, rationalism, discipline, and pragmatism.

The seal's reverse has a decentralized structure that unifies opposite elements. The eye in the triangle, representing spiritual unity and single vision, is situated above the pyramid, which symbolizes material diversity in its linear, multi-tiered structure. The pyramid is complete when the eye in the triangle remains in place; wholeness is achieved through the cooperation between these two elements. The reverse suggests an emblem of transformation and a movement toward wholeness and thus exemplifies the chief qualities of the new paradigm. According to Harman (1988, 163), the seal's reverse "clearly proclaims that the works of men (either individual character or external works) are incomplete unless they incorporate divine insight. This symbol is meant to indicate that the nation will flourish only as its leaders are guided by supraconcious intuition."

Ferguson and Harman identify the contemporary transitional interval with the American revolutionary period from which the Great Seal emerged. They cite the motto *Novus Ordo Seclorum* as evidence that the nation was consciously conceived as a momentous step in the evolution of the human species. From this vantage the American revolutionary period may be viewed as a theoretical paradigm shift in politics, government, and economics.

THE CONTEMPORARY TRANSITIONAL
PERIOD — THE NEW AGE

The difficulties we encounter during this age of transition are reflected in social disruption. Changes in our perception of marriage, divorce, family, sexuality, education, religion, and technology are most evident. These changes have created instability for many, resulting in feelings of confusion, anxiety, estrangement, loneliness, emptiness, and meaninglessness.

Rollo May (1976) has called attention to an increase in people's inability to feel and an avoidance of close relationships that he links to a larger cultural shift. He laments, "We are called upon to do something new, to confront a no-man's land, to push into a forest where there are no well-worn paths and from which no one has returned to guide us. This is what the existentialists call the anxiety of nothingness" (p. 2).

Some people are drawn to psychology to resolve emotional, mental, and spiritual problems. Psychology, reflecting Western culture's condition, is also in transition, redefining itself and returning to its primary business of an examination of consciousness.

HUMANISTIC PSYCHOLOGY

The growth and development of humanistic psychology support the investigation of human consciousness and attempt to resolve the personal and social dilemma facing humanity.

The general direction of humanistic psychology can be found in the observations of Charlotte Bühler, Gardner Murphy, Carl Rogers, Abraham Maslow, and Rollo May. Bühler (1971) emphasizes three aspects of the realization of one's potential—the importance of person-to-person relationships in education and psychotherapy, the acceptance of creativity as a basic human potential (not Freud's sublimation of neurotic traits), and the study of the person as a whole and open system. Murphy (1947) stresses positive growth-oriented personality traits over pathological aspects. Maslow (1977, 1978) believes that psychology should concern itself with values and asserts the importance to growth of "peak experiences," in which people are able to "witness the world" differently.

Humanistic and transpersonal psychology is, in part, an outgrowth of the contemporary cultural condition. The disruption in our collective and individual foundations has produced a period of instability during which neurotic symptoms are on the increase. Humanistically oriented researchers have focused on the current human condition in their attempts to resolve human and social dilemmas. Two suggested solutions, nearly universal among them, are to restore humanity to a condition of wholeness through the comprehension of its predicament and to help people utilize their unused or potential talents.

GROWTH EXPERIENCES

The process through which people can restore themselves to wholeness has been called self-actualization (Maslow, 1970; Rogers, 1965), peak and plateau experiences (Maslow, 1977, 1978), self-realization (Assagioli, 1973; Maslow, 1970), individuation (Edinger, 1973; Jacobi, 1974; Jung, 1973a; Progoff, 1969), self-transcendence (Frankl, 1966; Fromm, 1974), essentialization (Tillich, 1963), and personalization (DeChardin, 1964). All of these processes share some similarities and represent various aspects of growth experiences. The emotionally based peak experience, for example, develops toward the cognitive and serene plateau experience. From the plateau experience grows self-actualization, which is accomplished through a commitment to tasks outside of oneself. There are degrees of self-actualization, the highest of which is unselfish and universal.

Personalization and essentialization resemble self-transcendence, self-realization, and individuation. The latter three processes describe the fulfillment and maturation of the self to a whole state through which humanity's potential is fully manifested.

To Jung (1967), the self is the most important and the most central of archetypes; it represents wholeness. The self is the center of the totality of the psyche (Singer, 1977). It is the sum total of the individual's capacities (May, 1977). Its chief quality is the experience of synthesis, or the realization of individuality and universality (Assagioli, 1965).

THE MANDALA

Jung (1973a) used the mandala to represent the self. The mandala has been described as the mother of symbols and the matrix of symbolic systems (Argüelles and Argüelles, 1972). Because the variously named growth experiences are all aspects of a single process, the mandala can be used to describe them all.

Mandala is a Sanskrit word meaning circle. It denotes circular images that are not only drawn but painted, modeled, or danced. Argüelles and Argüelles (1972) suggest that the mandala's basic properties are center, symmetry, and cardinal points. Jung (1973a, 77) lists nine formal elements of mandala symbolism:

1. *Circular, spherical,* or *egg-shaped* formation.

2. The circle is elaborated into a *flower* (rose, lotus) or a *wheel*.

3. A center expressed by a *sun, star, or cross,* usually with four, eight, or twelve rays.

4. The circles, spheres, and cruciform figures are often represented in *rotation* (swastika).

5. The circle is represented by a *snake* coiled about a center, either ring-shaped (uroboros) or spiral (orphic egg).

6. *Squaring of the circle,* taking the form of a circle in a square or vice versa.

7. *Castle, city,* and *courtyard (temenos)* motifs, quadratic or circular.

8. *Eye* (pupil and iris).

9. Besides the tetradic figures (and multiples of four), there are also triadic and pentadic ones, although these are much rarer.

Mandalas are universal: they are found in ancient and contemporary cultures. The sand paintings of the Navajo creation myth and the Tibetan wheel of life, for example, were methods for entering the world of the gods (Eliade, 1959). The rituals of making or using them enabled their creators to orient themselves to eternal truths.

While ritual mandalas follow a relatively strict style and have a limited number of themes, individual mandalas express a wider range of motifs and symbolic allusions but generally conform to the fundamental elements. Just as ritual mandalas gave order and direction to the ancient cultures, Jung (1973a) holds that individual mandalas

> . . . have under certain circumstances a considerable therapeutic effect on their authors [that] is empirically proved and also readily understandable, in that they often represent very bold attempts to see and put together apparently irreconcilable opposites and bridge over apparently hopeless splits. Even the mere attempt in this direction usually has a healing effect, but only when it is done spontaneously. Nothing can be expected from artificial repetition or a deliberated imitation of such images. (p. 5)

Everything is related to the mandala's central point. It centers the individual and acts as a reference point from which to establish relationships. The mandala is an attempt to create order out of chaos.

Jung believed that the individuation process was the goal of psychic development and that the mandala, which represented it, was the preeminent symbol of our time.

THE SEAL'S REVERSE AS A MANDALA

Many national seals are circular, or mandala-like. In mandalas, the establishment of a central point to which everything is related creates order out of chaos, gives definition, and eliminates confusion. In a similar way, governments are constructed by establishing order and by acknowledging or determining the head of state.

There are obvious differences between the two sides of the Great Seal. The obverse of the seal contains the basic properties of a center; symmetry and the cardinal or chief points are readily established. The center of the seal's obverse falls in the throat area of the eagle. Analyzing the seal's obverse according to Jung's nine formal elements shows that it contains many aspects of the mandala:

1. It is circular.

2. The elements are arranged like a flower or wheel.

3. The center is the eagle's throat, and the wings, talons, head, tail, and banner can be likened to rays.

4. The obverse's elements are not in rotation, but they do suggest motion.

5. A coiling or spirallike effect is not pronounced but can be visualized.

6. The squaring of the circle can be found in the patterning of the eagle's wings and talons.

7. No castle or city and courtyard motifs are depicted.

8. The eagle has an eye.

9. The elements contain triadic and pentadic figures, such as the interlaced triangles above the eagle's head, which doubles as the top of a triangle with the arrows and olive branch serving as its base. The five-pointed star (pentadic) formation is found within the crest above the eagle's head, as well as the top of a pentagram with the eagle's wings, olive branch, and arrows serving as the four remaining points.

The seal's obverse is a well-defined mandala ordered around a central point. This could have some bearing on its immediate acceptance and use as the national seal. Early America may have attuned itself to the seal's obverse because it fulfilled an inner need for balance and structure, thus establishing a center that early Americans found meaningful.

The seal's reverse, on the other hand, does not contain as many of the fundamental mandalic elements. It is symmetrical. The cardinal points of north and south can be established, but east and west are less clear. With some difficulty, the center of the seal's reverse can be imagined near the center of the pyramid.

Using Jung's criteria for the mandala to evaluate the seal's reverse, we note the following:

1. It is circular.

2. It is not patterned after a flower or wheel.

3. Its center is vague and does not contain a sun, star, or cross.

4. It shows no evidence of rotation.

5. It has no spiral or coiling shape about the center.

6. It does not square the circle, but there is an indirect expression of this characteristic.

7. The pyramid can be likened to a castle.

8. It contains the single eye.

9. The pyramid has a triadic shape.

The seal's obverse could be described as an "embodied" or "affect" image (Richards and Richards, 1974, Campbell, 1973). That is to say, symbols are grounded in daily existence: they express meanings that give individual satisfaction and reflect the goals of our society. The eagle, shield, arrows, and olive branch speak directly to the feeling system and elicit an immediate response.

The reverse's elements are much less rooted in the American cultural experience, whether colonial or contemporary. The mystery and vagueness of these "disembodied" symbols conceal their meaning. The seal's reverse was not comprehensible to the America of the revolutionary period. Its gradual return to America's consciousness may indicate that our society is becoming more aligned with the values and goals expressed in the seal, or that the seal's symbols now communicate more directly to our emotions and focalize an element of the American public consciousness. In respect to the mandala's self-healing and centering capacities, the seal's reverse may be initiating a higher level of integration in the American consciousness, which, according to Jung, is the function of the mandalas.

Figure 17:
Sketch by one of Jung's patients
depicting the individuation process. The elements bear a striking
similarity to those found on the
seal's reverse. (Carl G. Jung, *Mandala Symbolism,* 1973.)

The eye in the triangle symbolizes the sun and consciousness and the father aspect of the deity. The pyramid or mountain may refer to the earth, unconsciousness, and the mother
deity. The sun (eye in the triangle) and earth (pyramid) are
separated, as is consciousness from unconsciousness. The
seal's reverse depicts the relationship between the physical
and psychological elements. The pyramid (physical) is unfinished. Its capstone (psychological) is unplaced. When the
capstone is set, the pyramid becomes whole and the psyche
is then linked with the body. The union of consciousness and
unconsciousness produces self-consciousness, from which
humanity becomes whole, individualized, and self-realized.

This union of opposites is an important mandalic element.
Jung's writings on mandala symbolism include a sketch that
contains elements of the sun and a hill or mountain (see
Figure 17). Jung referred to this sketch as depicting the individuation process. The similarities to the elements in the
seal's reverse are striking, and they support the contention
that the seal's reverse is a mandala depicting the individuation

process. The sun surrounded by a rainbow has the same meaning and basic structure of the eye radiating from the triangle. The mountain is a natural pyramid formation and it is found directly below the sun, just as the eye in the triangle appears above the pyramid.

June Singer (1977) examines the theme of the union of opposites. She believes we are entering a new era requiring a shift from the exclusively personal viewpoint to one that includes the transpersonal. It is a shift from an egocentric position toward a universal orientation; the new consciousness is our being in and of the universe, meaning also that the universe is in and of ourselves. We become not only the products of creation but co-creators. We are approaching a period in which we can now understand and make choices in the human evolutionary process. But we must recognize the weight of our responsibility in co-creating the world, a huge responsibility that many may wish to deny.

The elements in the seal's reverse can be likened to masculine (eye in the triangle as an active force linked to the sun) and feminine (pyramid holding, protecting, and nurturing the spirit) values. The New Order of the Ages is a union of masculine and feminine virtues; it is androgynous. In its broadest sense, androgyny can be defined as the one that contains two; namely, the male (andro-) and the female (-gyne). Androgyny may be the oldest archetype of which we have any experience; humans have an innate sense of a primordial cosmic unity existing in oneness before any separation was made. True change in the androgyny begins primarily within the psychic structure of the individual. The seal's reverse represents the archetypal androgyne. As such, it can be understood as a symbolic system, or archetype, delineating the philosophy of the transitional period, or New Age.

Argüelles and Argüelles (1972) identify two fundamental mandala types: the cosmic fortress and the mandala as the transmutation of demonic or negative forces. The seal's reverse is more like the latter type. The transmutation process unfolds in the act of setting the eye in the triangle atop the pyramid, whereby consciousness connects with unconsciousness, bringing about self-consciousness or wholeness. The demonic force in this instance is the stone structure of the incomplete (i.e., not whole) pyramid, which is not conscious of itself, or self-realized. The partial pyramid's union with its opposite (the eye in the triangle, or consciousness) develops wholeness, self-actualization, and self-healing.

The Great Pyramid

One might also see the pyramid as a fortress or castle and therefore link Argüelles's first type to the seal's reverse. At least one element is missing from the fortress model—the center that is protected by the fortress. The seal's designers, Hopkinson (1778) and Barton (1782), meant the pyramid to be a depiction of the Great Pyramid of Giza. Other historians have confirmed this. Comparing the pyramid on the seal's reverse to the Great Pyramid at Giza may resolve the difficulty in locating the center of the reverse.

Figure 18 shows the Great Pyramid's internal structure. About one-third up from its base is the King's Chamber. Although the King's Chamber is not located in the actual center of the Great Pyramid, it is considered the central and most important chamber in the Great Pyramid, for it is the area in which the candidate was "raised" for initiation, during which he transmuted his lower physical nature and became self-realized or whole. Ferguson (1980, 81–82) refers to the King's Chamber in the Great Pyramid as the "transcendent center." Also worth noting is the fact that the central vertical meridian going from the top of the Great Pyramid to the center of its base passes through the entrance to the King's Chamber. The pyramid in the seal's reverse is placed at something less than a three-quarter angle, therefore the site of the King's Chamber in the seal's reverse would be moved more to the right, to allow for the angular vantage.

The Great Pyramid viewed from the top shows that the King's Chamber does not fall in the center (see Figure 19) but closer to the entrance to the King's Chamber.

Research on the Great Pyramid has disclosed a possible chamber below the entrance of the King's Chamber (see Figure 20) (Dolphin, 1979, confirmed by Japanese archeologists in 1987). The center of the seal's reverse may coincide with this suspected chamber in the Great Pyramid.

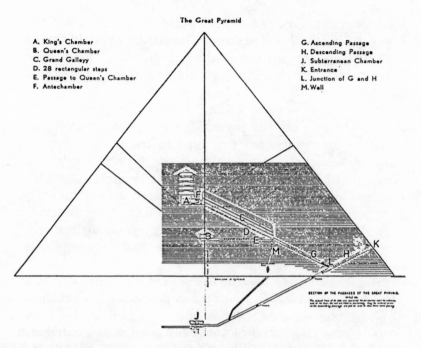

The Great Pyramid

A. King's Chamber
B. Queen's Chamber
C. Grand Galleyy
D. 28 rectangular steps
E. Passage to Queen's Chamber
F. Antechamber

G. Ascending Passage
H. Descending Passage
J. Subterranean Chamber
K. Entrance
L. Junction of G and H
M. Well

Figure 18:
An internal side-view of the Great Pyramid showing passageways and chambers. (Peter Tompkins, *Secrets of the Great Pyramid,* 1971.)

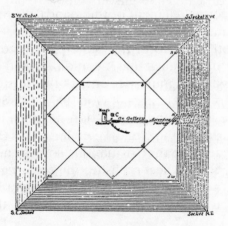

Figure 19:
An internal top-view of the Great Pyramid showing location of the King's Chamber. (Peter Tompkins, *Secrets of the Great Pyramid,* 1971.)

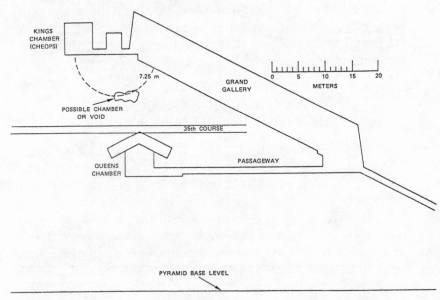

Figure 20:
Recent research suggests the location of a possible new chamber in the Great Pyramid. (*Applications of Modern Sensing Techniques to Egyptology,* 1977.)

Squaring the Circle

Jung's sixth formal element of the mandala is the squaring of the circle. Squaring the circle is one of the most important archetypal motifs that form the basic patterns of dreams and fantasies, so fundamental that it could be called the archetype of wholeness. Its significance makes the "quaternity of the one" the basis for all images of God (1973a, 4). Some theorists believe there is a strong connection between true pyramids and the squaring of the circle. Peter Tompkins (1971, 197), for example, argues that the "pyramid is so designed that for all practical purposes it accomplishes the squaring of the circle. The pyramid's base is a square whose perimeter is equal to the circumference of a circle whose radius is the Pyramid's height."

Mainstream America has long identified with the seal's obverse, and no wonder, for it more readily expresses the mandalic pattern and hence describes self-realization. The seal's reverse embodies fewer of the mandalic elements, but growth in public consciousness about its meaning suggests that it is embodying more of America's consciousness and is becoming an affect image (see page 80).

THE GROWTH EXPERIENCE
SYMBOLIZED IN THE SEAL'S REVERSE

The seal's reverse incorporates the basic ideology of humanistic and transpersonal psychology. It symbolizes the process through which the individual achieves self-realization and wholeness. Its two basic elements, the eye in the triangle and the pyramid, are opposites that are in the process of being transformed into a whole. When these two elements, representing consciousness and unconsciousness, are linked, self-consciousness begins to emerge. This result describes Maslow's peak experience, in which the dichotomies, polarities, and conflicts of life are transcended or resolved, and movement toward the perception of unity and personal fusion and integration occurs (Maslow, 1977, 65–66).

The eye in the triangle and the pyramid might also represent, respectively, linear or analytic thought (often associated with the left hemisphere of the brain) and intuitive thought (right hemisphere). Linking the eye in the triangle and the pyramid transforms two foreign and opposite elements into something new, whole-brain knowing. The seal's reverse could thus symbolize this transformational aspect of a new paradigm that furthers the evolutionary development of the human species.

The seal's reverse can be seen as describing the concept that the universe can be perceived as an integrated and unified whole. It may express the peak experience and the more advanced stages of integration (self-transcendence, self-realization, and individuation). The seal's reverse might represent the unification of the psychological and physical dimensions of being that transform the many (consciousness/unconsciousness, male/female, active/perceptive, positive/negative) into one and that also transform fragmentation into wholeness, thus helping to resolve transitional consciousness.

At least on the symbolic level the Founding Fathers may have realized that if America were to succeed it must embody all the characteristics symbolized on the seal's obverse and reverse. Their vision was expressed in the symbols and mottoes of a two-sided national emblem, of which only the seal's obverse has been utilized legally and recognized nationally as America's coat of arms.

The Founding Fathers embodied their vision of America in a symbol. Understanding the power of symbols is therefore of great importance if we are to comprehend this vision.

THE POWER OF SYMBOLS

To behavioristic psychologists symbols are man-made signs whose meanings are cultural and transitory. Positivists perceive symbols as fables and myths that are invented to entertain. Many see symbols as unreal and therefore insignificant. Some writers in the humanistic tradition, however, see myths, symbols, and archetypes as significant forces in the psyche rather than sources of historical or factual knowledge of the objective world.

Humanity's cultural deficiency in developing symbolic and mythological systems is regarded by transpersonal psychology as a factor contributing to our contemporary disintegrative state. Symbols cultivate wholeness and are a bridge between the conscious and unconscious, resulting in the process of individuation and self-realization. The symbol contains both conscious and unconscious elements and relates to the entire psychic system; it can therefore be assimilated by consciousness with relative quickness.

Concerning the symbols and the self, Carl Rogers (1965, 497) asks: "Is the self primarily a product of the process of symbolization? Is it the fact that experiences may not be directly experienced, but symbolized and manipulated in thought, that makes the self possible? Is the self simply the symbolized portion of the experience?"

If the self is a product of its symbolization, and no contemporary symbol systems exist, experiencing the self would prove to be problematical and could result in both alienation and fragmentation of the personality.

The humanistic tradition suggests that symbols originate not in the intellect but in the irrational depths of the psyche (Read, 1955). "Symbols cannot be produced intentionally. . . . They grow out of the individual or collective unconscious and cannot function without being accepted by the unconscious dimension of our being" (Tillich, 1958, 43).

Paul Tillich believes that only the symbol can convey our ultimate concerns. The symbol participates in that to which it points, opens up levels of reality, and unfolds unknown dimensions of the soul.

Symbols are spontaneous products of the archetypal psyche that cannot be discovered or manufactured. They are often seen as carriers of psychic energy. Without symbolic life the ego is alienated from its suprapersonal source, and falls victim to a kind of cosmic anxiety. The ultimate goal of Jungian psychotherapy is to make the symbolic process conscious.

Erich Neuman (1974) views the symbolic experience as a primary existence, and as such every symbol and archetype has a specific content, and "when the whole of a man is seized by the collective unconscious, that means his consciousness too" (p. 85).

June Singer (1973) cites the power of the symbol to attract and lead the individual on the way to becoming what he or she is capable of becoming. "That goal is wholeness, which is integration of the parts of his personality into a functioning totality. Here conscious and unconscious are united around the symbols of the self" (p. 385).

Rollo May (1976, 153) regards the original meaning of symbol as "drawing together." This definition echoes Singer's process of integration and wholeness. The individuation process facilitates a homogeneous being (Jung, 1953) and leads us to the missing part of the whole person. It heals our alienation from life (Edinger, 1973).

Jung (1973a) is also convinced that the unconscious forms symbols by way of revelation, intuition, or dreams. He thinks that slowly evolving symbol formations are responsible for the development of cultural ideas and behavior. Symbols are the formative agents of communities: they supply the psychological and the organizational foundations of social life (Jung, 1973b; Odajynk, 1976).

Joseph Campbell (1973) believes that the most important effect of a living mythological symbol is an energy-released and directing image that awakens and guides humanity, one that is conducive to participation in the life and purpose of a functioning social group.

Symbols grow and die (Tillich, 1958). Our era is one during which time-honored symbol systems have collapsed (Campbell, 1972). Richards and Richards (1974) describe our period as one of increasing isolation and estrangement, where the person is no longer the central concern. They note that self-actualization and self-realization acquire authentic meaning when they are embodied and disclosed in one's life. When the image of the whole person is not found in the life and concrete actions of the individual it is a disembodied image.

Similar to the embodied image is the *affect image*. This is a term applied to a living mythological symbol by John W. Perry (Campbell, 1973):

> It is an image that hits one where it counts. It is not addressed first to the brain, to be there interpreted and appreciated. On the contrary, if that is where it has to be read, the symbol is already dead. An "affect image" talks directly to the feeling system and immediately elicits a response. . . . When the vital symbols of any given social group evoke in all of its members responses of this kind, a sort of magical accord unites them as one spiritual organism. (pp. 89–90)

To sum up, symbols play a central role in the integrating of the personality. They direct us to the center of our being. They are objects pointing to subjects. Symbols lead us to the missing part of the whole and relate us to our original totality, healing and mending our alienation from life. The lack of affect images and the presence of disembodied images create an existential vacuum. The absence of a symbol system leaves communities without formative agents, which supply the psychological and organizational foundations of social life, thereby increasing instability and anxiety.

Chapter 5

A Symbolic Analysis of the Seal's Reverse

THE two central symbols on the seal's reverse, the eye in the triangle and the pyramid, are interpreted differently in historic and esoteric traditions. The historic tradition regards only the views of William Barton and Charles Thomson as having authority, whereas the esoteric tradition accepts a broader range of interpretations.

THE SINGLE EYE

Barton and Thomson in 1782 interpreted the eye in the triangle as "many signal interpositions of Providence in favor of the American cause" and cited the use of the single eye as the "all Seeing Eye of the Deity." It was placed on the fifty-dollar bill in 1778. The single eye was a well-established artistic convention for an "omniscient Ubiquitous Deity" in the medallic art of the Renaissance. Du Simitière, who suggested using the symbol, collected art books and was familiar with the artistic and ornamental devices used in Renaissance art.

The single eye, alone or in a triangle, was used extensively by Freemasons and other secret societies. It is the probable cause for Professor Norton's reference to the seal's reverse as a "dull emblem of a Masonic fraternity" (Hunt, 1909, 55).

In 1776, Du Simitière first proposed the eye in the triangle.

It later reappeared in Barton's designs in 1782, and Charles Thomson gave it final approval. Thomson was a biblical scholar and as such may have been aware of several biblical references to the single eye. For example, Matthew 6:22 states, "If therefore, thine eyes be single thy whole body shall be full of light." An almost identical phrase can be found in Luke 11:34.

Du Simitière, Barton, and Thomson also could have been aware of the single eye motif in Egyptian symbolism. To the ancient Egyptians, the right eye symbolized the sun and the left eye the moon. The seal of 1782 depicted the right eye, but after Benjamin Lossing submitted his designs in 1856, the left eye was used. If Barton knew of the Egyptian conventions, his use of the right eye may have symbolized the sun. To the Egyptians the sun was the creative aspect of the Deity, just as the eye in the triangle symbolized divine providence to them.

The single eye also has been identified with the third or spiritual eye and therefore with clairvoyance. The esoteric tradition relates the single eye to the inner light, intuitive power, illumination, and the philosopher's stone (Hall, 1947). Jung compares the eye to the mandala, the structure of which symbolizes the center of order in the unconscious. Thus, the eye can also represent God.

THE TRIANGLE

Many religions possess trinities or triads, for example, Christianity's Father, Son, and Holy Spirit; Judaic cabalism's Kether, Cochma, and Binah; ancient Egypt's Osiris, Isis, and Horus; and Hinduism's Brahma, Vishnu, and Shiva.

There may be a deep-seated tendency to organize temporal or developmental events into threefold patterns. To Freud, psychological development was seen in three states—oral, anal, and genital—while Edinger perceived the development of consciousness as ego, self, and ego-self axis. Alfred North Whitehead distinguished three stages in the natural learning process: romance, precision, and generalization. Hegel understood the historical process from the threefold cyclic pattern of thesis, antithesis, and synthesis. This is identical to what Rosicrucians refer to as the "law of the triangle" (Lewis, 1941).

Joseph Campbell's monomythic process is also threefold: separation, initiation, and return. The individuation process bears many similarities to the monomyth. Edinger conjectures that the trinity archetype symbolizes the individuation process, whereas the quaternity stands for its completed state. "Three is the number for ego-hood; four is the number for wholeness, the Self. But since individuation is never truly complete, each temporary state of completion or wholeness must be submitted once again to the dialectic of the trinity in order for life to go on" (1973, 193).

Officially, the eye in the triangle symbolized "the many signal interpositions of Providence in favor of the American cause" (Barton and Thomson, 1782). All the aforementioned interpretations are in harmony with this reading. Spiritual vision, illumination, intuitive power, and the philosopher's stone all refer to and describe providence—or, as the Freemasons would say, "the All Seeing Eye of God," the "Supreme Great Architect of the Universe" (*The Bible*, Masonic edition, 1960).

THE PYRAMID

According to Barton and Thomson, the pyramid signifies "Strength and Duration." William Barton first suggested a pyramid for the seal's reverse. In 1778 Francis Hopkinson had placed a pyramid on a continental fifty-dollar bill. Barton's interest in paper credit probably made him aware of the design.

Patterson and Dougall reveal the inspiration for Hopkinson's design:

> As to the pyramid, there was widespread interest in Egypt and things Egyptian in the eighteenth century, and in the Library Company of Philadelphia there was a detailed work entitled "Pyramidagraphia" [by John Greaves] which would have been available to both Hopkinson and Barton. This work included a drawing of the "first pyramid," which was stepped, did not come to a complete point, and had an entrance in the center on the ground level—a detail found also in Hopkinson's design. (1976, 531)

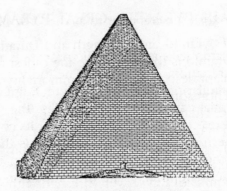

Figure 21:
Entrance to the Great Pyramid as
depicted by Sir John Greaves.
(*Pyramidographia,* 1736.)

Greaves's and Hopkinson's designs show obvious similarities (see Figure 21. See also Figure 11, page 52.) The entrance to Greaves's pyramid, however, is not at ground level, as stated by Patterson and Dougall, but on a pile of rubble chiseled from the pyramid.

John Greaves was an Oxford mathematician and astronomer. In 1638 he tried to establish the dimensions of the planet from measurements of the Great Pyramid. He believed that the Great Pyramid was built to record the dimensions of the earth and to furnish imperishable standard linear measure. Sir Isaac Newton used Greaves's measurements of the Great Pyramid in a rare paper, "A Dissertation upon the Sacred Cubit."

John Greaves's research also gave the mathematical calculations that "pyramidologists" used in their system of interpretation. His work is the basis for cabalistic interpretations of the pyramid's measurements. The ultimate origins of the pyramid on the seal's reverse could be interpreted as carrying cabalistic interpretations, for Greaves thought that the Great Pyramid itself contained such meanings.

If Greaves is Hopkinson's source, then the pyramid on the seal's reverse is ultimately the Great Pyramid of Giza.

SEAL'S PYRAMID = GREAT PYRAMID

What type of pyramid did "Strength and Duration" refer to? The Great Pyramid is thought to be the oldest and largest in the world, an apt description of the immortality alluded to by Barton and Thomson.

When the Tiffany Company cut a new die for the seal, Theodore F. Dwight, chief of the Bureau of Rolls and Library, inquired of the company: "Is the pyramid drawn to the scale of the Great Pyramid? . . . If I am correctly informed the veritable pyramids of Egypt were finished with smooth lines, and that the steps, or indentations now appear, because the surface stones have been removed, if such is the case your representation need no correction in that respect."

Tiffany answered Dwight that, "The reverse of the Pyramid is drawn to the scale of the Great Pyramid: the side seen in perspective to the right means the East, this view being desired" (Patterson and Dougall, 1976, 253).

Another similarity between the Great Pyramid and the seal's pyramid is their incompleteness, for neither have capstones set in place. The seal's capstone is suspended above the pyramid. We do not know whether the Great Pyramid of Giza ever had a capstone. Sometimes the ancients did not complete their temples or monuments, to symbolize the imperfection of the mundane world. Another possibility is that a capstone once existed but was stolen or removed. The capstone of the Great Pyramid was missing centuries before Greaves, Hopkinson, and Barton completed their renderings, and the probability is high that they used the Great Pyramid as their model.

THE GREAT PYRAMID: TOMB, TEMPLE, OR GENERATOR?

Tradition holds that the Great Pyramid was a tomb for the pharaoh Khufu. Although it may have been a burial monument, other purposes have been ascribed to it. For centuries, the treasures it reportedly contained have been of an informational nature.

Contemporary "pyramidologists" (Coville and Nelson, Tompkins, Valentine, West) have proposed that the Great Pyramid was a theodolite for surveyors, an almanac of the ages, an astronomical and astrological observatory, and a geodetic and geographic landmark. There are also many who believe that the pyramid's shape is an "energy" generator (Coville and Nelson, Flanagan, Toth and Nielson, Russell, Valentine). They theorize that the pyramid shape may act as a huge resonating cavity that is capable of focusing the rays of the cosmos like a giant lens, affecting the molecules or crystals of any object in the path of the beam of focused "energy."

A significant number of esoteric writers (Paul Brunton, Manly P. Hall, H. Spencer Lewis, and Peter Tompkins) identify the Great Pyramid as a temple of initiation. In this temple, neophytes became aware of the heavenly worlds by undergoing a series of initiations that made them realize their personal and collective unconscious processes.

THE FUNCTION OF ARCHETYPES

The seal's reverse is an emblem composed of symbols derived from archetypes. The archetype is a preformed pattern of thinking and is the "dominant" of the collective unconscious. Archetypes are not abstract universal images but dynamic living organisms that promote change in the depths of the human psyche.

Jung's analysis of the psyche's strata details the process by which the unconscious goal orientation of the mind evolves from primal chaos, takes form in the preformed patterns of functioning, and resolves itself in words and ideas.

Jung terms the first stratum of the psyche the psychoidal level, in which the psyche and the natural world are fused together in an undifferentiated mass. The psyche has yet to achieve a distinctly psychological quality. The psychoidal level corresponds to the microcosmic representation of the primal chaos in the universe. At the psychoidal level instinct and archetype are fused and the psyche is able to catch reflections of the surrounding macrocosm.

Jung's second stratum is the collective unconscious. The archetype is the structural element in the unconscious. It expresses itself in metaphors with some part of its meaning remaining unknown.

Archetypes mediate the primal chaos in the psychoidal stratum of the psyche. They are vehicles through which order is transmitted from the collective unconscious into the personal unconscious. The archetype acts as an ordering principle or constellating hub, around which experiences reappear again and again.

The more primary the archetype, the deeper it lies within the unconscious. The scantier the archetype's basic design, the more possibilities of development are contained within it, and the richer their meanings.

Jung lists the principle archetypes affecting human thought and behavior as the self, the persona (the role-playing personality), the shadow (the unconscious), the anima (feminine characteristics), the animus (masculine characteristics), the wise old man (spirit who provides guidance in a meaningful direction), the earth mother (who brings forth all life from herself), and the child (the young undeveloped aspect of the personality). The self is the central archetype or archetype of wholeness. Progoff regards the self as the archetype of archetypes. "The Self may be understood as the essence and aim and the living process by which the psyche lives out its inner nature" (1973b, 91). The individuation process is also archetypal, allowing human potential to be developed into a unique personality.

Becoming conscious of the archetype produces a state of alienation, because "something is added to the individual's consciousness which ought really to remain unconscious, that is, separated from the ego" (Singer, 1973, 81).

THE PYRAMID AND THE ARCHETYPAL MOUNTAIN

The pyramid symbol on the seal's reverse may be derived from the mountain archetype. Frankfort and Frankfort (1963) explain the mountain/pyramid relationship: "In Egypt the

Creator was said to have emerged from the waters of chaos and to have made a mound of dry land upon which he could stand. This primeval hill, from which creation took its beginning, was traditionally located in the sun temple at Heliopolis, the sun god being in Egypt most commonly viewed as the creator. . . . Hence the royal tomb was given the shape of a pyramid which is [the] Heliopolitan stylization of the primeval hill" (pp. 30–31).

Mircea Eliade (1959, 12) locates the sacred mountain (where heaven and hell meet) at the center of the world and lists some cultural expressions of this cosmology. "According to Indian beliefs, Mount Meru rises at the center of the world, and above it shines the polestar. The Ural-Altaic peoples also know a central mountain Sumeru, to whose summit the polestar is fixed. Iranian beliefs hold that the sacred mountain Haraberezaiti (Elburz) is situated at the center of the earth and is linked with heaven. The Buddhist population of Laos, North of Siam, know of Mount Zinnalo, at the center of the world." In another work, Eliade compares the Ziggurat to the cosmic mountain. We can liken the polestar over the mountain to the eye in the triangle over the pyramid.

Erich Neuman's *The Great Mother* (1970) provides historical, cultural, and psychological interpretations of the mountain and its meaning to the psyche. Neuman relates mountain symbolism to mother symbolism. The central symbolism of the feminine is the vessel, which fulfills the function of containing, protecting, and nourishing.

The center of the vessel, or the belly, is linked to the mountain symbol. Below the belly is the womb, which is attached to the cave. The mountain serves to protect the cave, which is connected to a series of related archetypes, one of which is the coffin. The transformation process within the feminine scheme begins in the lowest level—the darkness, night, underworld, the unconscious. It proceeds to the belly, heart-breast, and mouth areas.

The elements of mountain, cave, and coffin symbolism can be traced in the design of the Great Pyramid. We can identify the Great Pyramid with the mountain, the cave with the King's Chamber, and the coffer with the coffin.

Some Rosicrucian and Freemason groups assert that the

Great Pyramid was used to conduct rites of initiation. The Master Mason's third-degree ritual parallels the initiation process the temple neophyte underwent before he became a master of the spiritual plane. The third degree of the great Masonic initiation was said to have been conducted in the Great Pyramid. The candidate purportedly was placed in the coffer in the King's Chamber for three days, whence he left his physical body to visit the spiritual world where will and character were tested. If the candidate succeeded, he gained a view of the microcosm and insight into personal destiny. Returning from the spiritual realms, the candidate was reborn into the physical world and set about realizing his potential by rendering service. According to Freemasonry, the highest privilege of the human being is work in the service of the Divine Architect (Brunton, 1965).

Jung (1970, 97) connects the mountain symbolism to "the goal of the pilgrimage and ascent, hence it often has the psychological meaning of the self." Ascending the mountain is analogous to the process of knowing oneself. Knowing oneself is becoming conscious of the unconscious, or of uniting opposites.

It is from the union of opposites, in the alchemical process, that the philosopher's stone emerges. This stone is triune in substance and in part regenerative. The shapes, forms, and symbols used to depict the alchemical process are repeated in the mountain, cave, coffin, and rebirth themes. The process of rebirth and transformation is depicted repeatedly and universally by the same symbols, which indicate that their source is an archetypal process. The archetypal processes of rebirth, transformation, self-realization, and individuation are growth experiences that cultivate wholeness. They promote growth through labor, attention, and devotion, and are analogous to the work done by the Master Mason in the service of the Divine Architect.

MYTHOLOGY

For the most part the contemporary world identifies myths with fairy tales and legends. The humanistic tradition sees myths not as sources for the accumulation of an objective knowledge of man's external world but rather as a significant force in the human psyche. A myth's content is not seen as valuable from anthropological, intellectual, and sociological perspectives. The events and time tables of a myth are often paradoxical and contradictory. The humanistic view of myths places the greatest emphasis not on their historic value, but on their description of humanity's psychological development.

MYTHS AND ARCHAIC SOCIETY

Archaic society regarded myths as a pattern of actions (or rituals) performed by deities, heroes, and ancestors. By imitating the actions of these figureheads, people found their identity. Human behavior was therefore a ceaseless repetition of gestures initiated by others. The repetition of such gestures allowed the participant to enter the world of gods, heroes, and ancestors in which mundane time did not exist. Any act that was not an "imitation" was meaningless and considered unworthy (Eliade, 1959).

Birth, adolescence, marriage, and death were considered a series of initiations during which humans experienced the essential oneness of the individual and the group. Individual meaning was found in the group, and the group's meaning was taken from the actions performed by the gods, as described in myths. This dependency on myth and derivative ritual processes was not only significant to the individual, it influenced the development of ancient cities, palaces, temples, and tombs.

MODERN SOCIETY AND MYTHS

Modern society has no exemplary models to follow, for contemporary people associate themselves with history and not the cosmos. We find the past unworthy of imitation and ritual meaningless. Gods, heroes, and ancestors offer little. Technology has become the center of contemporary man's adulation. With no patterns of behavior to imitate, twentieth-century humanity must turn inward to acquire meaning, destiny, and purpose. A living mythological symbol awakens and guides the energies of human life. Feinstein and Krippner's (1988) recent research notes that "while no one can reliably predict what new myths will come to dominate in the coming decades, a remarkably diverse group of candidates from the 'New Fundamentalism' to the 'New Age' can be seen vying for the cultural spotlight" (p. 219).

Several mythic systems can be read into the elements on the seal's reverse. The process that best illustrates the mythological meaning of the seal's reverse was evolved by the late Joseph Campbell. Campbell refers to the hero process as the monomyth, which consists of three stages: separation, initiation, and return. The monomyth is similar to the ordering principle of the archetypal psyche that analytic psychology uses.

The three stages of initiation, separation, and return describe the evolution of the hero (Campbell, 1972, 1973). During separation, the individual rejects the social order and retreats inward or regresses. He reassesses his beliefs and moves toward the center of his being. The second stage marks a clarification of his difficulties and the encountering of dark and terrifying forces. The candidate is victorious over them and feels fulfilled, harmonized, and whole. In the return, the third stage, the hero is reborn into the physical world and applies the knowledge he has gained to the world he lives in. He rejects his self-serving and self-centering tendencies and shares his "treasure" (new awareness) with the rest of society. The hero has become self-actualized, and he dedicates himself to a task outside of himself, serving society.

Campbell regards the monomythic process as identical to the experience of the schizophrenic. The monomythic process is a natural way of healing alienation, as are the processes of self-realization, self-transcendence, and individuation. Archaic people learned the essential oneness of the individual within the group through the rites of passage. Since contemporary society has rejected the external rites of passage, modern humanity may internalize these, suggesting that the monomyth is essential—as are self-realization, self-transcendence, and individuation—to the continued health of the psyche.

THE SEAL'S REVERSE AS A MONOMYTH

The seal's reverse depicts the separation state in the separation of the eye in the triangle from the pyramid. There is not only a separation between the pyramid and its capstone but also a difference in their substance. The pyramid is made of stone, rock, and earth—and represents the unconscious. The capstone is made of an immaterial substance—light or spirit—and is conscious.

The pyramid exemplifies the initiation stage of the monomyth. As a tomb, it is the pharaoh's final resting place and the place where he is initiated into the afterlife. As a temple, it is the house of initiation, in which the candidate confronts the world of darkness and enters the world of spirit. By passing the tests of the elements, the candidate is initiated into the realm of higher consciousness, from which he perceives the oneness of all things spiritual and material.

After successfully completing the initiation process, the candidate is reborn or transfigured. The return, in the monomyth process, is represented by the hero joining the single eye in the triangle—the deity—to the many-tiered pyramid. The one becomes the many, that is, the capstone joins the multiple-stoned pyramid. The capstone is returned to the pyramid through the hero's labor. The successful completion of this task is a service the hero renders to society. The supreme deed of the hero is to make known his experience of perceiving the unity in multiplicity. By sharing his firsthand knowledge and the fruits of his labor, he helps to carry the human spirit forward, restoring meaning and purpose to culture.

Thus, through the struggle of linking consciousness (the eye in the triangle) and unconsciousness (the pyramid), the individual becomes self-realized and centered. The struggle of placing the capstone is symbolic of the internal struggle the psyche undergoes in making order out of chaos. The tops of mountains were considered the center of the universe. To reach its summit and remain there, as the hero does in completing the pyramid, means that the individual has become centered and is at one with the cosmos.

Chapter 6

The American Vision
and Its Fulfillment

YE ARE BRETHREN

The vision of the Founding Fathers can be described in the biblical phrase, "Ye are Brethren," and Thomas Jefferson expressed this philosophy more openly than the other Founding Fathers: "The fulfillment of Jeffersonian equality was not postponed to a future state when all economic classes would disappear and each would be rewarded according to his needs. Equality was first and foremost a biological fact" (Boorstin, 1963, 105).

In essence he was espousing the foundational philosophy of Freemasonry, "the brotherhood of man and the fatherhood of God." In other words (aside from the sexism of the language), all humans are brothers, in effect we are one world, one people. The symbols and mottoes found on both sides of America's seal also reflect Jefferson's philosophical ideals that all humanity is one.

The obverse or front side of the American Seal depicts the bald eagle holding a scroll upon which is emblazoned *E Pluribus Unum*, meaning "Out of many, one." *E Pluribus Unum* conveys the same meaning as "Ye are brethren." Although the Latin motto alludes to the union of the thirteen colonies into one nation, it can also refer to the manyness of the material world being transcended by the unity of the spiritual world.

Charles Thomson explains the motto *Novus Ordo Seclorum* as a reference to the new American era that commenced in 1776. This new era was America's republican form of government, which signaled a New Age in the sense that people were becoming more able to rule themselves rather than submitting to tyranny. The New Order was the brotherhood of humanity, in which all humans were equal. *Annuit Coeptis* boldly announces that God favored the founder's vision, that it had a spiritual dimension.

ESOTERIC BELIEFS ABOUT AMERICA'S DESTINY

If some of the Founding Fathers were influenced by the esoteric tradition, the Freemasons, Rosicrucians, and Illuminati's visions of America's destiny are significant. While it is difficult to ascertain what esoteric Freemasonry had to say on this subject, the beliefs of the Rosicrucians and Theosophists (whose philosophy and teachings mirrored Freemasonry) are spelled out in some detail.

Theosophists and Rosicrucians (Heindel, 1956; Heline, 1941) believe that America was the thirteenth step in evolution. The occult tradition states that man, the prodigal son, is journeying from unconsciousness to cosmic consciousness through a series of root races. By adding up the Lemurian race (originating in the Indian Ocean), the seven sub-races of the Atlantean race, and the five present sub-races of the Aryan race (originating in India), we come to the number 13 (1 + 7 + 5 = 13). The thirteenth race is expected to mother a sixth sub-race, which in turn will foster the sixth root race. By the year A.D. 2600, the seeds of the sixth root race will have germinated, and a great part of America's destiny will have been fulfilled.

As America nurtures the beginnings of the sixth root race, other nations are evolving toward their own destinies. Occultists such as H.P. Blavatsky, Rudolf Steiner, Edgar Cayce, and others believe that Russia is paralleling America's evolution. Russia's spiritual contribution is not expected to manifest until the fourth millennium. They believe that Russia and America will unite in the next two millennia, with earlier attempts being only temporarily successful.

The Theosophical and Rosicrucian traditions hold that every nation has a spiritual destiny guided by a hierarchy of beings using all ethical means of manifesting the divine plan through the will of the nation's leaders. It was England's destiny, for example, to be the mother of nations. Her empire was slowly and painfully disassembled while she learned the lessons of selflessness and service to mankind. America repeats similar lessons in the Near and Far East while she struggles to uphold the aspirations of Thomas Paine's belief that "The world is my country, All mankind are my brethren, To do good is my religion, I believe in one God and no more" (Cousins, 1958, 394).

The dawning of a new age is a spiritually potent era. Many of the ideas, beliefs, and hopes for the Aquarian age will be expressed first in their initial forms. The coming decades will see many altruistic endeavors attempted. It is from these beginnings that the seeds will be sown for the New Age.

The emergence of world brotherhood could be expedited in the merging of the western hemisphere, the union of America, Canada, and Mexico being the most likely first step. The union of South America with North America would link the remaining western hemisphere, as Jefferson wished.

The union in the eastern hemisphere will take more time, but its success is inevitable. Great Britain and Europe could act as the cement for the two hemispheres. The only way the efforts toward world union could remain permanent would be through peaceful negotiations. All methods using force would destroy its longevity.

According to the Rosicrucians and Theosophists, supporting the divine plan are great beings referred to as masters of the physical and spiritual planes. The evolution of America owes much to the seed thoughts of four masters—Kuthumi, El Morya, Rogoczy, and Djwal Kul. Some of the founders of America may have been consciously or unconsciously students of these teachers, just as some contemporary Americans are pupils of these masters. In fact, the motto of the hierarchy of world teachers is identical with America's destiny—the brotherhood of man and the Fatherhood of God.

Most nations may prefer their independence, but wars, economic survival, and environmental problems will inevitably persuade nations to pursue the objective of one world. Having accomplished world union, America's spiritual destiny will have been fulfilled.

A BLUEPRINT FOR DESTINY

The Great Seal of America not only describes the destiny of the American nation and its people, but also refers to all humanity on this planet. The seal's reverse expresses the vision of self-transformation. From the union of spirit and matter, a new being—a transformed being—is created that is more than the sum of its parts. God favors this process (*Annuit Coeptis*) for it expresses the New Order of the Ages (*Novus Ordo Seclorum*). Few would see this process or vision as anything but positive, but how can such a vision be realized?

The past two decades have seen the growth of various groups and techniques which encourage self-transformation and self-realization. Their goal is to unite the mortal physical body with its spiritual counterpart, thus producing a higher awareness of one's self with respect to the universe. This self-realization process is the foundation for determining individual purpose. In other words, the elevation of consciousness provides a perspective that allows one to glimpse a higher order of things, which, in turn, indicates the role of the individual in society.

America's Great Seal may be seen as a blueprint for the elevation of consciousness. It says, in part, that first we must transform ourselves before we can change the world, and that it is during the process of self-transformation that we can catch a glimpse of what part we are to play in national and global transformation.

Since 1776 America has been the leader in realizing the goal of self-government. The spirit of America has successfully followed the path of initiation toward global vision. America has served not only its people but the world. America is responsible for regenerating the spirit of "liberty, equality, and fraternity" begun during the French Revolution. America can be seen as having had the wisdom of becoming a nation of various nationalities: its "melting pot" philosophy has been one of its great strengths. America has had the wisdom to engrave "In God We Trust" and *Annuit Coeptis* on its currency, suggesting that all the money in the world has no power behind it unless it is supported by divine providence.

PLANETARY REGENERATION

There are also powers at work within the United States that have debilitated its spirit. These forces dominate American culture today. We see these forces at work daily in the way we poison the earth, water, and air. We cannot continue this wholesale destruction of our nation and planet without the severe consequences we are just beginning to experience.

How did we get the environment in this hellish predicament? It is a result of the old paradigm scenario in which Mother Earth is conquered and dominated, just as the male species has dominated the female for the past few millennia. This belief system rejects the importance of spirit and puts its full confidence in the ledger. But, has man "conquered" nature? If he has, he had better prepare himself for what Mother Earth has in store. Nature will cleanse itself regardless of national boundaries and powerful governments.

Fortunately, there is a growing number of world citizens who do not view the earth as an object to be controlled and conquered. They see the earth as a living entity embodying a spiritual life force that nourishes the physical earth and is responsible for the planet's equilibrium. It is not necessary to confront or conquer this life force: cooperating can bring a more positive response. This philosophy exemplifies the new paradigm in that it embraces the reality of both material and spiritual worlds.

America has led the world into a new age of democratic consciousness. But America has also led the way in industrializing and polluting the planet. This planetary destruction must be curtailed immediately if we are to prevent the total collapse of our planetary life force. Again, America must take the lead in reversing this diabolical predicament.

DOING IT NOW

But what can we do now? Step one is service to others, or volunteerism. You can help clean up the environment. You can work on legislation to prevent continued pollution. You can lobby for a cleaner earth or even run for office.

As you volunteer your services to transform the earth, you need to decide on the extent of your service. Do you want to work on these problems in your neighborhood, or focus your attention on city and state matters? You may feel the need to venture into a regional problem or one that is national, continental, or global.

It is not enough to undertake a service project. The project should be brought to a successful conclusion, and it is this struggle that transforms an ideal into an actuality. The result of bringing to birth a positive change in the world's ecological systems is a physical rebirth or regeneration of our planet.

The fourth step in the journey towards transforming the self is the accumulation of the wisdom of the process of regeneration, and the knowledge that right action under the right circumstances gives birth to a new consciousness leading to global vision.

As Americans we have an important job to do. We must transform ourselves before we can successfully transform our planet. We must take the role of leadership in supporting programs that will return the earth to its former healthy balance. We must set tougher standards and see that they are met. Don't depend on the government to do it. It cannot wait until public officials have the character to support the life systems on this planet rather than the industrial world's needs. Americans, because of their form of government, have the capacity to return the earth to environmental balance and global health. It is inherent in our nature, as it is inherent in the very symbol that represents the American nation—the Great Seal.

Whatever you choose to do, do it quickly. The world stands on the brink of global revolution. We can consciously choose an enlightened course ushering in a New Age of planetary harmony and peace. The League of the Iroquois chose that course hundreds of years before America's founders lived this vision. America is destined to lay the foundation of world peace and global unity. We can encourage this process by remembering that we are not the people of a city or state. We are not the people from the east or west coasts of America. We are people from the planet earth. We are earth people. "Ye are Brethren."

Afterword

COMPLETING THE GREAT SEAL OF THE UNITED STATES OF AMERICA

It is my contention that it is absolutely necessary to complete what our Founding Fathers began: finish America's Great Seal. They did not envision a nation based upon material principles only! They knew that such a nation would lose its finest resources. My wife, Zoh, and I lobbied from 1976 to 1986 for the completion of our nation's Coat of Arms and the cutting of the die of the reverse of the Great Seal. Six years of that decade (1981–1986) were devoted to the creation and pursuit of legislation. During the 97th Congress (1982) we worked with Senator Mathias (R., Md.) in an effort to get a Presidential proclamation passed. S.R. 394 (sponsored by Mathias, and cosponsored with Goldwater, Nunn, and Pell) would have directed the State Department, the Keeper of the Seal, to cut a die of the reverse. The proclamation went through senior staff sign-off on the eve of the Great Seal's Bicentennial, June 20, 1982. The Legal Council's Office struck language that was pertinent to the cutting of the reverse die from the document, leaving only the proclamation of the week of June 20, 1982, as Great Seal Week.

One objection to the resolution was that the proclamation would affect a standing law, which, under most circumstances, must be changed by Congressional agreement. Title 4 of the United States Code (1934) says that "the seal heretofore used" shall be the seal of the United States (referring only to the obverse.) The proclamation was in obvious conflict with this code. The other prohibiting factor cited was that there was no language regarding appropriations ($13,000) for the striking of the die. We learned with the senators, the hard way. All subsequent legislative efforts were written to amend Title 4 of the United States Code, which would complete the official seal of the United States. Language regarding appropriations for the act was included as well.

During the years following 1982, Senator Charles McC. Mathias (R., Md.) successfully sponsored the Great Seal Act of 1983 (S.R.1177), managing to get unanimous support in the Committee on Foreign Relations where the bill was assigned during the 98th Congress. The Great Seal Act passed without objection before the full Senate on August 2, 1984. It failed to be introduced in the House.

Mathias, known for his love of American history, reintroduced the Great Seal Act of 1985 (S.R.726) to the 99th Congress in hopes that the House of Representatives would do as well. Waiting for the House action, the Great Seal Act was never brought before the full Senate for a third consideration.

Senator Barbara Mikulski, then Representative Mikulski (D., Md.), introduced a companion bill during the 98th Congress. It was only in the 99th Congress as H.R.1670, the Great Seal Act of 1985 (Judiciary Committee-Civil and Constitutional Rights), that the bill received a subcommittee hearing. The bill was never reported out to the full judiciary prior to the end of the Congressional year. The bill was never brought before the full 99th or 100th Congresses.

In our recent discussions with Senator Mikulski about responsoring the Great Seal Act and identifying a House sponsor, she focused on the need for grassroots support in order to demonstrate a national interest in the issue.

Let's show our national interest.

WHAT YOU CAN DO NOW!

Write to Senator Barbara Mikulski, 320 Hart Senate Office Building, Washington, D.C. 20520; (202) 224–4654, and urge her to sponsor legislation for the completion of our nation's Coat of Arms, or simply, to introduce the Great Seal Act of 1989.

Write to your own senator or representative and ask them to join Senator Mikulski in this historic legislative effort. Remind them that it was the intention of our Founding Fathers that both of these symbols, the obverse and the reverse, represent the United States and validate the President's signature. Refer to the fact that the legislation passed the Senate unanimously in 1982 and 1984, but never had the opportunity to be voted upon by the full House of Representatives. You can reach your State's Congressional members at their local offices or write to:

Senator _____
The U.S. Senate
Washington, D.C. 20510

Congressional Representative _____
The U.S. House of Representatives
Washington, D.C. 20510

HOW MUCH DO OUR LETTERS MEAN?

It may surprise you to know that when a bill is under discussion, your senators and representatives consider what you have to say. Some offices take their constituent's letters to the floor as proof of citizen concern and others weigh the overall poundage of mail pertinent to a given issue. Some offices equate one citizen letter to the voices of 100 to 3,000 other citizens. Every letter counts.

MORE THAT YOU CAN DO TO HELP STRIKE A DIE OF THE GREAT SEAL'S REVERSE

At the time of this writing, the presidential elections had just been held. Many new seats in Congress, and hence committees and subcommittees, had not been assigned. By the time you read this book, however, your state senators and representatives will be able to get the lists of the subcommittees where eventual legislation will, in all probability, be referred.

Ask your congressional representatives' offices to get a list of the Senate Committee on Foreign Relations and the House Subcommittee on Civil and Constitutional Rights of the Judiciary Committee. A list of committee members will be useful once the legislation has its sponsors and active pursuit of the bills are underway.

The Role of the Subcommittee

Each member of a subcommittee should be sent letters. Send only legible, hand-written or typed letters. Do not send xeroxed or computer-generated forms. Send numerous letters to the Chairperson. He or she decides what bills are scheduled for review. No matter how wonderful a piece of legislation, if no one tells the members of Congress about it, it may go unnoticed. If the bills' sponsors are not on the subcommittee where the bills are referred, it is even more difficult to ensure committee interest and the scheduling of a hearing.

Legislative bills move from subcommittees to full committees and then to the floor of the House or Senate for a full congressional vote. When a piece of legislation passes out of a subcommittee unanimously or with minimal opposition, it is almost always assured passage by the full committee and subsequent passage before the Senate or House of Representatives.

Most of the work that goes into getting legislation passed occurs while a bill is in subcommittee. First, it must be brought to the attention of the subcommittee and other influential members of Congress. Lobbyists solicit support for additional cosponsors (other senators and representatives) as well as approval by the full committee members where applicable.

THE GREAT SEAL NETWORK

We are creating a Great Seal Network that will announce the changing status of the effort to complete our Great Seal, and that will ask your assistance at each stage of the legislative process via a newsletter and via national radio on **The Dr. Bob Show**, airing nationally on the American Radio Networks and regionally on the Atlantic Coast Radio Network.

To participate in this phase of seeing our Founding Fathers intentions fulfilled, write to:

Great Seal Network (GSN)
4801 Yellowwood Avenue
Baltimore, MD 21209

You can also call (301) 367–7300 and give the office your name, address and phone number, and best time to reach you.

Specify if you need to be called back. Long-distance calls will be returned collect.

Completing the Great Seal means turning national attention to its reverse at last. As we absorb the symbolism of its all-seeing eye and Great Pyramid, we will reawaken the archetype, drawing it from the unconscious to the active consciousness of our nation. We can expect an American self-realization, a quantum awakening, a recognition of America's spiritual destiny.

My wife, Zoh, and I send forth this volume as an invitation to each of you to help fulfill this vision.

Robert R. and Zohara M. Hieronimus
June 20, 1989

Appendix 1

National and Regional Environmental, Agricultural, Animal, and Human Rights Groups and Services

This directory was prepared by Zoh Meyerhoff Hieronimus, Director of the Ruscombe Mansion Community Health Center, in Baltimore, MD. Those desiring to serve our nation and world environmentally may select an organization to assist them toward such goals.

ENVIRONMENTAL/NATURAL RESOURCES

Acres USA
10008 E. 60th Terrace
Kansas City, MO 64133
(816) 737–0064

American Farmland Trust
1920 N. Street NW
Washington, DC 20036
(202) 659–5170

American Rivers Conservation
   Council
323 Pennsylvania Avenue, SE
Washington, DC 20003
(202) 547–6900

American Rivers
801 Pennsylvania Ave., SE,
   Suite 303
Washington, DC 20003
(202) 547–6900

Audubon Naturalist Society of
the Central Atlantic States
8940 Jones Mill Road
Chevy Chase, MD 20815
(301) 652–9188

Baltimore Resources
602 Woodbine Terrace
Towson, MD 21204
Attn: Bonnie & Robin Raindrop
(301) 339–7716

Bio-Integral Resource Center
PO Box 7414
Berkeley, CA 94707
(703) 885–9683

Center for Environmental
Education
1725 DeSales St., NW
Washington, DC 20036
(202) 429–5609

Center for Renewable Resources
1001 Connecticut Ave., NW,
Suite 530
Washington, DC 20036
(202) 466–6350

Chemical and Radiation Waste
Litigation Reporter
1519 Connecticut Ave., NW,
Suite 200
Washington, DC 20036
(202) 462–5755

Citizens Energy Council
Box 285
Allendale, NJ 07401
(201) 327–3914

Citizens for a Better Environment
536 West Wisconsin Ave.,
Suite 502
Milwaukee, WI 53203
(414) 271–7280

Clean Air Council
Juniper and Locust Street,
2nd Floor
Philadelphia, PA 19107
(215) 545–1832

Clean Water Action Project
733 15th Street, NW, Suite 1110
Washington, DC 20005
(202) 638–1196

Coalition for the Environment
6267 Delmar Boulevard
University City, MO 63130

Conservation International
1015 18th Street, NW, #1000
Washington, DC 20077–5979
(202) 429–5660

The Cousteau Society
930 W. 21st Street
Norfolk, VA 23517
(804) 627–1144

Earth First!
Rt. 1, Box 250
Staunton, VA 24401

Earth Save Foundation
PO Box 949
Felton, CA 95018-0949
Attn: John Robbins
(408) 479–7355

Ecological Illness Law Report
PO Box 1796
Evanston, IL 60204
(312) 256–3730

Energy Conservation Coalition
1725 I Street, NW, Suite 601
Washington, DC 20006
(202) 466–5045

The Environmental Action
 Foundation
724 Dupont Circle Building
Washington, DC 20036
(202) 659–9682

Environmental Action, Inc.
1525 New Hampshire Ave., NW
Washington, DC 20036
(202) 745–4871

Environmental Defense Fund
257 Park Ave. South
New York, NY 10010
(212) 686–4191

Environmental Defense Fund
1616 P Street, NW
Washington, DC 20077–6048
(202) 387–3500

Environmental Law Institute (ELI)
1346 Connecticut Ave., NW,
 Suite 600
Washington, DC 20036
(202) 452–9600

Friends of the Earth
530 7th Street, SE
Washington, DC 20003
(202) 543–4312

Grassroots International
PO Box 312
Cambridge, MA 02139
(617) 497–9180

Greenpeace USA
1611 Connecticut Ave., NW
Washington, DC 20009
(202) 462–1177

Health and Energy Learning
 Project
236 Massachusetts Ave., NE, #506
Washington, DC 20002
(202) 543–1070

Human Ecology Action League
PO Box 1369
Evanston, IL 60204
(312) 864–0995

INFACT
National Field Campaign Office
PO Box 3223
South Pasadena, CA 91030
(617) 742–4583

INFORM
381 Park Ave.
New York, NY 10016
(212) 689–4040

Institute for a Future
2000 Center Street
Berkeley, CA 94704
Attn: Larry Ephron
1–800–441–7707
(415) 524–2700

International Wildlife Coalition
1807 H St., NW, Suite 301
Washington, DC 20006
(202) 347–0822

League of Conservation Voters
320 4th Street NE
Washington, DC 20002
(202) 547–7200

National Coalition Against the
 Misuse of Pesticides
530 7th Street
Washington, DC 20003
(202) 543–5450

National Recycling Coalition, Inc.
45 Rockefeller Plaza, Rm. 2350
New York, NY 10111
(212) 675–1920

National Wildlife Federation
1412 16th Street, NW
Washington, DC 20036
(202) 797–6895

National Wildlife Federation-
    Natural Resource Law Clinic
Fleming Law Building, Room 160
Boulder, CO 80309
(303) 492–6552

National Resources Defense
    Council
122 East 42nd Street
New York, NY 10168
(212) 949–0049

Natural Resources Defense
    Council
90 New Montgomery St.
San Francisco, CA 94105
(415) 777–0220

New Forests Fund
731 Eighth St., SE
Washington, DC 20003
(202) 547–3800

Project Earth
PO Box 1031
Evergreen, CO 80439
Attn: Adam Trombley
(303) 670–3344

Rainforest Action Network
300 Broadway
San Francisco, CA 94133
(415) 398–4404

Renew America: The State of the
    States Report
1001 Connecticut Ave., NW,
    Suite 638
Washington, DC 20036
(202) 466–6880

Sierra Club
PO Box 7603
San Francisco, CA 94120–9826
(415) 776–2211

Sierra Club Legal Defense Fund
2044 Fillmore Street
San Francisco, CA 94115
(415) 567–6100

Solar Age or Ice Age? Bulletin
(*The Survival of Civilization*
    Crisis Report)
Hamaker-Weaver Publishers
Box 1961
Burlingame, CA 94010
Attn: Don Weaver
(415) 342–0329

Union of Concerned Scientists
26 Church Street
Cambridge, MA 02238
(617) 547–5552

United States Public Interest
    Research Groups (USPIRG)
215 Pennsylvania Ave., SE
Washington, DC 20003
(202) 546–9707

Washington Environmental
    Council
80 South Jackson
Seattle, WA 98104
(206) 623–1483

HEALTH/FOOD/AGRICULTURE

American Agriculture Movement
100 Maryland Ave., NE
Suite 500A, Box 69
Washington, DC 20002
(202) 544-5750

American Farmland Trust
1920 N Street, NW
Washington, DC 20036
(202) 659-5170

Americans for Safe Food
PO Box 66300
Washington, DC 20035
(202) 332-9110

Center for Science in the Public
Interest
1501 16th Street, NW
Washington, DC 20036
(202) 332-9110

Chemical and Radiation Waste
Litigation Reporter
1519 Connecticut Ave., NW,
Suite 200
Washington, DC 20036
(202) 462-5755

Community Nutrition Institute
2001 S Street, NW, Suite 530
Washington, DC 20009
(202) 462-4700

Consumer Energy Council of
America
2000 L Street, NW, Suite 320
Washington, DC 20036
(202) 659-0404

Consumers United for Food
Safety
PO Box 22928
Seattle, WA 98122

The Cornucopia Project for
Rodale Press
35 E. Minor St.
Emmaus, PA 18049
(215) 967-5171

Environmental Policy Institute
218 D Street, SE
Washington, DC 20003
(202) 544-2600

Food and Drug Administration
5600 Fishers Lane
Rockville, MD 20857
(301) 443-1544

Food Irradiation Response
Newsletter
Box 5183
Santa Cruz, CA 95063

Food Research and Action Center
(FRAC)
1319 F Street, NW
Washington, DC 20004
(202) 393-5060

Health and Energy Learning
Project
236 Massachusetts Ave., NE, #506
Washington, DC 20002
(202) 543-1070

Health Policy Advisory Center
17 Murray St.
New York, NY 10007
(212) 267-8890

Institute for Food and
Development Policy
1885 Mission St.
San Francisco, CA 94118
(415) 668-2090

League for Urban Land
Conservation
1150 Connecticut Avenue, NW,
12th Floor
Washington, DC 20036
(202) 457-1039

National Coalition to Stop Food
Irradiation (NCSFI)
PO Box 590488
San Francisco, CA 94159
(415) 566-2734

Northwest Coalition for
Alternatives to Pesticides
PO Box 1393
Eugene, OR 97440
(503) 344-5044

Organic Crop Improvement
Association
PO Box 729A
White Oak Road
New Holland, PA 17557

Organic Food Producers
Association of North America
PO Box 31
Belchertown, MA 01007

People Food and Land
Foundation
34756 Weymiller
Tollhouse, CA 93667
(209) 855-3710

People for Responsible
Management of Radioactive
Waste
3 Whitman Drive
Denville, NJ 07834

Pesticides Action Network—
North America Regional
Center
Pesticide Education Action
Project
PO Box 610
San Francisco, CA 94101
(415) 771-7327

Physicians for Social
Responsibility
639 Massachusetts Avenue
Cambridge, MA 02139
(617) 491-2754

Planned Parenthood Federation
of America, Inc.
810 Seventh Ave.
New York, NY 10019
(212) 541-7800

Public Citizen Health Research
Group
2000 P Street NW
Washington, DC 20036
(202) 872-0320

The Ruscombe Mansion
Community Health Center
4801 Yellowwood Avenue
Baltimore, MD 21209
(301) 367-7300

US Department of Agriculture
14th and Independence Ave., SW
Washington, DC 20250
(202) 447-8732

ENERGY

Center for Renewable Resources
1001 Connecticut Avenue, NW,
Suite 530
Washington, DC 20036
(202) 466-6350

Citizen Energy Council
Box 285
Allendale, NJ 07401
(201) 327-3914

Coalition for the Environment
6267 Delmar Boulevard
University City, MO 63130
(314) 727-0600

Energy Conservation Coalition
1725 I Street, NW, Suite 601
Washington, DC 20006
(202) 466-5045

National Center for Appropriate
   Technology
PO Box 3838
Butte, MT 59702
(406) 494-4572

Nuclear Information and
   Resource Center
1346 Connecticut Avenue, NW,
   4th Floor
Washington, DC 20036
(202) 296-7552

Nuclear Regulatory Commission
Washington, DC 20553
(301) 492-7000

Solar Lobby
1001 Connecticut Avenue, NW,
   Suite 530
Washington, DC 20036
(202) 466-6350

TRANET
PO Box 507
Rangeley, ME 04970
(207) 864-2252

POLITICAL POLICY/EDUCATION/
COMMUNITY SERVICE

American Civil Liberties Union
132 W. 43rd Street
New York, NY 10036
(212) 944-9800

American Friends Service
   Committee
1501 Cherry Street
Philadelphia, PA 19102
(215) 241-7000

American Red Cross
1730 E. Street, NW
Washington, DC 20006
(202) 737-8300

Amnesty International USA
322 Eighth Avenue
New York, NY 10117-0389
(212) 807-8400

Catalyst
14 E. 60th Street
New York, NY 10022
(212) 759-9700

Congress Watch
215 Pennsylvania Ave., SE
Washington, DC 20003
(202) 546-4996

Common Boundary
7005 Florida Street
Chevy Chase, MD 20815
(301) 652-9495

Common Cause
2030 M Street, NW
Washington, DC 20036
(202) 833-1200

Community Information
Exchange
1120 G Street, NW, 9th Floor
Washington, DC 20036
(202) 628-2981

Consumer H-E-L-P Clinic
2000 L Street, NW, Suite 307
Washington, DC 20052
(202) 676-4879

Great Seal Network (GSN)
4803 Yellowwood Ave.
Baltimore, MD 21209
(301) 367-7300 or 664-7628

Highlander Research and
Education Center
Route 3, Box 370
New Market, TN 37820
(615) 933-3443

Human Rights Internet
1338 G Street, SE
Washington, DC 20003
(202) 543-9200

Institute for Policy Studies
1901 Q Street, NW
Washington, DC 20009
(202) 234-9382

Interhelp
PO Box 331
Northampton, MA 01061

Interspecies Communication
273 Hidden Meadow Lane
Friday Harbor, WA 98250

Institute of Noetic Sciences
475 Gate Five Road, Suite 300
Sausalito, CA 94965
(415) 331-5650

League of Women Voters
1346 Connecticut Avenue, NW
Washington, DC 20036
(202) 429-1965

National Organization for
Women
425 13th Street, NW
Washington, DC 20003
(202) 347-2279

National Organization for
Women's Legal Defense and
Education Fund
132 West 43rd Street
New York, NY 10036
(212) 354-1225

National Center for Youth Law
1663 Mission St., 5th Floor
San Francisco, CA 94103
(415) 543-3307

Native American Rights Fund
1506 Broadway
Boulder, CO 80302
(303) 447-8760

Nuclear Weapons Freeze
Campaign
600 West 28th Street, #106
Austin, TX 78705
(512) 469-0208

Physicians for Social
Responsibility
639 Massachusetts Avenue
Cambridge, MA 02139
(617) 491-2754

Planetary Citizens
325 Ninth Street
San Francisco, CA 94103
(415) 626-6992

Planned Parenthood Federation
of America
810 Seventh Avenue
New York, NY 10019
(212) 541-7800

Project HOPE
PO Box 250
Milwood, VA 22646
(804) 837-2100

Public Interest Clearing House
200 McAllister Street
San Francisco, CA 94102
(415) 557–4014

SANE—The Committee for a
Sane Nuclear Policy
711 G Street, SE
Washington, DC 20003
(202) 546–7100

SEVA Foundation
108 Spring Lake Drive
Chelsea, MI 48118

UNICEF Committee
331 East 38th Street
New York, NY 10016
(212) 686–5522

Washington Council of Agencies
1309 L Street, NW
Washington, DC 20005
(202) 393–3636

Worldwatch Institute
1776 Massachusetts Ave., NW
Washington, DC 20036
(202) 452–1999

ANIMAL RIGHTS/FARM ANIMALS

American Anti-Vivisection
Society
801 Old York Road
Jenkintown, PA 19046
(215) 887–0816

American Society for the
Prevention of Cruelty to
Animals
441 East 92nd Street
New York, NY 10128
(212) 876–7700

American Vegan Society
501 Old Harding Highway
Malaga, NJ 08328

Animal Legal Defense Fund
333 Market Street
San Francisco, CA 94105
(415) 495–0885
or: 205 East 42nd Street
New York, NY 10017
(212) 818–0130

Animal Protection Institute of
America
6130 Freeport Blvd.
PO Box 22505
Sacramento, CA 95822
(916) 731–5521

Animal Rights International
Box 214
Planetarium Station
New York, NY 10024

Association of Veterinarians for
Animal Rights
530 E. Putnam Ave.
Greenwich, CT 06830

Compassion in World Farming
20 Lavant St.
Petersfield, Hants, England

The Culture and Animals
Foundation
3509 Eden Croft Drive
Raleigh, NC 27612
(919) 782–3739

Defenders of Wildlife
1244 19th Street, NW
Washington, DC 20036
(202) 659–9510

Farm Animals Reform Movement
PO Box 70123
Washington, DC 20088
(301) 530–1737

Friends of Animals, Inc.
11 West 60th Street
New York, NY 10023
(212) 247–8077

The Fund for Animals
200 W. 57th Street
New York, NY
(212) 246–2096

Food Animals Concern Trust
PO Box 14599
Chicago, IL
(312) 525–4952

Humane Farming Association
1550 California St., Suite 6
San Francisco, CA 94109
(415) 485–1495

Humane Society of the United
   States (HSUS)
2100 L Street, NW
Washington, DC 20037
(202) 452–1100

In Defense of Animals
21 Tamal Vista Blvd.
Corte Madera, CA 94925
(415) 924–4454

International Fund for Animal
   Welfare
PO Box 193
Yarmouth Port, MA 02675

International Society for Animal
   Rights, Inc.
421 South State St.
Clarks Summit, PA 18411
(717) 586–2200

International Wildlife Coalition
1807 H Street, NW
Suite 301
Washington, DC 20006
(202) 347–0822

National Anti-Vivisection Society
100 East Ohio Street
Chicago, IL 60611
(312) 787–4486

National Humane Education
   Society
211 Gibson St., NW
Suite 104
Leesburg, VA 22075
(804) 777–8319

National Wildlife Federation
1412 Sixteenth Street, NW
Washington, DC 20036–2266
(202) 797–6800

North American Vegetarian
   Society
PO Box 72
Dolgeville, NY 13229
(518) 568–7970

People for the Ethical Treatment
   of Animals (PETA)
PO Box 42516
Washington, DC 20015
(202) 726–0156

Progressive Animal Welfare
   Society
(PAWS)
PO Box 1037
Lynwood, WA 98046
(206) 743–3845

San Francisco Vegetarian Society
1450 Broadway
San Francisco, CA 94109
(415) 775–6874

Trans-Species Unlimited
PO Box 1553
Williamsport, PA 17703
(717) 322–3252

The Wilderness Society
1400 I Street, NW
Washington, DC 20005
(202) 842–3400

World Wildlife Fund
1250 24th Street, NW
Washington, DC 20037
(202) 293–4800

REFERENCES

Diet for A New America, John Robbins, Still Point Publishing, Walpole, NH, 1987.

Food Irradiation, Who Wants it? Tony Webb, Tim Lang, and Kathleen Tucker, Healing Arts Press, Rochester, VT, 1987.

Good Works (A Guide to Careers in Social Change), Joan Anzalone, Ed., Dembner Books, New York, 1985. (*Good Works* lists over 600 organizations and includes a comprehensive bibliography about additional resource directories as well as describing organizations' objectives and projects.)

Pesticide Alert (A Guide to Pesticides in Fruits and Vegetables), Lawrie Mott and Karen Snyder, Sierra Club Books, San Francisco, CA, 1987.

Secrets of the Soil, Christopher Bird and Peter Tompkins, Harper & Row, 1989.

Appendix 2

Chronological History of the Great Seal

First Congress, July 4, 1776	Congress appoints a committee to design America's Coat of Arms or Great Seal.
1776–1782 June 20, 1782	The Great Seal is adopted. Three committees deliberate before adopting the Great Seal as a two-sided or two-imaged Coat of Arms composed of an obverse seal (eagle and shield) and a reverse (pyramid with eye in triangle).
1782 September 16	George Washington uses only the obverse die in a treaty document for the better treatment and subsistence of POWs.
1825	Die cut of the Great Seal's obverse (Massi die), reverse seal is neglected.
1841	Die cut of the Great Seal's obverse (Throop die), reverse seal is neglected.
1877	Die cut of the obverse seal (Baumgarten die), reverse seal is neglected.
1882	Charles A. Totten suggests that a commemorative medal be struck showing the complete Great Seal in honor of its centennial.
1884 July	$1,000 appropriated to strike commemorative medal.
1885	Die cut of obverse seal (Tiffany die), reverse seal is neglected.
1904	Die cut of the obverse seal (Zeitler die), reverse seal is neglected.

1935	F.D. Roosevelt places image of complete Great Seal on the back of the one dollar bill.
1976	The State Department publishes its excellent historical work (Patterson and Dougall) *The Eagle and the Shield* in honor of the Great Seal's bicentennial (1982).
1976 June	President Gerald Ford uses Robert R. Hieronimus's research in the opening of the centennial safe during the Nation's Bicentennial.
1976 Dec. 28	Robert R. Hieronimus is asked to the White House to discuss the history and meaning of the two Great Seals of America.
1981 October	Robert R. Hieronimus receives his doctorate for his work on the history and meaning of the Great Seal of the United States, "An Historical Analysis of the Reverse of the American Great Seal and Its Relationship to the Ideology of Humanistic Psychology."
1981 December	Dr. Robert R. Hieronimus and Zohara Meyerhoff Hieronimus are asked to the White House to discuss the history and meaning of the Great Seal.
Dec., 1981, to May, 1982	Dr. and Mrs. Hieronimus assist in the creation of language and pursuit of a Presidential Proclamation to authorize the State Department (Keeper of the Seal) to complete the Great Seal by having die cut of its reverse image (pyramid with eye in triangle), and its use as intended by our Founding Fathers.
1982 April	The Department of Interior requests that Dr. and Mrs. Hieronimus create a brochure on the Great Seal for their distribution. The Hieronimuses prepared and paid for 10,000 brochures, which were distributed during the Great Seal's bicentennial celebration at Independence Hall in Philadelphia.
1982 May 18	S.R. 394, Senator Warner (for himself, Goldwater, Nunn, and Pell) calls for the completion of the Great Seal by having a die cut of its reverse.
1982 June 15	The State Department celebrates the Great Seal's bicentennial and the postal service releases its first-day issue of the obverse seal embossed in honor of the Great Seal's bicentennial.
1982 June 18	S.R. 394 passes in the Senate unanimously.

1982 June 18–19	S.R. 394 goes to Senior Staff sign-off at the White House (Dole, Duberstein, Fuller, Harper, Rollins approve). President's counsel's office (Fred Fielding) removes from proclamation language on the cutting of the Great Seal's reverse die, leaving only language that calls for the week of June 20, 1982, to be called Great Seal Week. Fielding cites (a) absence of appropriation language and (b) reference to appropriate laws not included.
1982 June 20	Bicentennial celebration at Independence Hall in Philadelphia, Dr. Robert Hieronimus addresses public on history and meaning of Great Seal.
1982 July 20	Senator Charles McC. Mathias enters Dr. Hieronimus's speech into the Congressional Record (Legislative day July 12).
1983 February	Senator Mathias's office draws up new legislative language to amend Title 4 of the United States Code (standing law of 1934 to be amended).
1983 February	Congresswoman B. Mikulski agrees to sponsor legislation in the House.
1983 April 28	Senator Mathias introduces Great Seal Act of 1983, S.R. 1177.
1983–1984	S.R. 1177 assigned to Subcommittee on Foreign Relations.
1984 June 19	S.R. 1177 passes out of committee with unanimous approval.
1984 August 2	S.R. 1177 passed unanimously by the Senate.
1984 August	Congresswoman Mikulski introduces legislation in House, referred to Judiciary, Civil and Constitutional Rights (Chairman Don Edwards).
1984 September	Chairman Edwards says there won't be time this Congress to address bill.
1985 February	Senator Mathias introduces S.R. 726.
1985 February	Congresswoman Barbara Mikulski introduces H.R. 1670.
1985 May	Congressman Edwards (Chairman, Subcommittee Civil and Constitutional Rights) assures speedy passage of bill.
1986 February 13	Letter from Chairman Edwards saying thank you for information.

| 1986 February 13 | Letter from Senator Lugar, Chairman of Senate Foreign Relations, indicating approval of bill in principle. |
| 1986 August 14 | Dr. and Mrs. Hieronimus provide testimony for the House Judiciary subcommittee regarding the cutting of a die for the seal's reverse. |

Bibliography

Aldridge, A. O. *Benjamin Franklin and Nature's God*. Durham, NC: Duke University, 1967.

Allen, P. *A Christian Rosenkreutz Anthology*. New York: Rudolph Steiner Publications, 1968.

Anderson, J. *New Book of Constitutions of the Ancient and Honorable Fraternity of Free and Accepted Masons*. n.s.: C. Ward and R. Chandler, 1738.

Argüelles, J., and Argüelles, M. *Mandala*. Boulder, CO: Shambala, 1972.

Ashe, G. *The Ancient Wisdom*. London: Macmillan, 1977.

Assagioli, R. *Psychosynthesis*. New York: Viking Press, 1965.

Assagioli, R. *The Act of Will*. New York: Viking Press, 1973.

Bauman, R. F. Claims vs. Realities: The Anglo-Iroquois partnership. *Northwest Ohio Quarterly*, 1960, *32*(2), 87–101.

Beauchamp, W. M. *A History of the New York Iroquois, Now Commonly Called the Six Nations*. Port Washington, NY: I. J. Friedman, 1962.

The Bible, King James Version.

The Bible, Masonic edition. Chicago: The John A. Hertel Co., 1960.

Bindrim, P. Facilitating peak experiences. In H. A. Otto & J. Man (Eds.), *Ways of Growth*. New York: Viking Press, 1969.

Bird, C. *The Divining Hand: The Five Hundred Year Old Mystery of Dowsing*. New York: E. P. Dutton, 1979.

Boorstin, D. *The Lost World of Thomas Jefferson*. Boston: Beacon Press, 1963.

Borg, W. R., and Gall, M. D. *Educational Research*, 3rd ed. New York: Longman, 1979.

Breasted, J. H. *The Dawn of Conscience*. New York: Charles Scribner's Sons, 1968.

Brown, J. L. P. *A Bibliography of the Iroquois Indians.* New York: Columbia University, 1903.

Brown, W. A. *Facts, Fables, and Fantasies of Freemasonry.* n.s.: William Adrian Brown, 1968.

Brunton, P. *A Search in Secret Egypt.* London: Arrow Books, 1965.

Bühler, C. Basic theoretical concepts of humanistic psychology. *American Psychologist,* 1971, *26,* 378–386.

Burnett, E. C. Charles Thomson. *Dictionary of American Biography,* 1933, *12,* 481–482.

Campbell, J. *The Hero with a Thousand Faces.* Princeton, NJ: Princeton University Press, Bollingen Series 17, 1972.

Campbell, J. *Myths to Live By.* New York: Bantam Books, 1973.

Campbell, R. A. *Our Flag or the Evolution of the Stars and Stripes.* Chicago: H. E. Lawrence, 1890.

Carey, G. W. *13—The mystery of the divine number revealed.* Los Angeles: n.p., n.d.

Carr, L. *The Social and Political Position of Women among the Huron-Iroquois Tribes.* Salem, MA: Salem Press, 1884.

Carr, W. G. *Pawns in the Game.* Glendale, CA: St. George Press, 1970.

Case, P. F. *The Great Seal of the United States, Its History, Symbolism and Message for the New Age.* Santa Barbara, CA: J. F. Rowny Press, 1935.

Champlin, J. D., Jr. The Great Seal of the United States: Concerning some irregularities in it. *The Galaxy 23,* May 1877, 691–694.

Child, I. L. *Humanistic Psychology and the Research Tradition; Their Several Virtues.* New York: John Wiley & Sons, 1973.

Cigrand, B. J. *Story of the Great Seal of the United States or History of American Emblems.* Chicago: Cameron Amberg, 1903.

Clark, R. T. R. *Myth and Symbol in Ancient Egypt.* New York: Grove Press, 1960.

Clift, W. B. Symbols of wholeness in Tillich and Jung. *International Journal of Symbology,* 1976, 7(2), 45–52.

Clymer, E. M., and Ricchio, P. P. *Our Story of Atlantis, or the Three Steps.* Quakertown, PA: Beverly Hall Corp., 1972.

Cobb, W. H. *The American Challenge.* Beverly Hills, CA: Privately published by the author, 1943.

Cohen, F. Americanizing the White Man. *American Scholar,* 1952, *21*(2), 177–191.

Cohen, L. K., Ed. *The Legal Conscience: Selected Papers of Felix S. Cohen.* New Haven: Yale University Press, 1960.

Colden, C. *The History of the Five Indian Nations Depending on the Province of New York in America.* Ithaca, NY: Cornell University Press, 1958.

Costrell, E. Personal correspondence between Edwin Costrell, Chief Historical Studies Division, U. S. State Department and the writer, June 14, 1973.

Cousins, J. *Two Great Theosophist Painters: Jean Delville, Nicholas Roerich.* Theosophical Publishing House, 1925.

Cousins, N. *In God We Trust.* New York: Harper & Bros., 1958.

Coville, D. H., and Nelson, D. J. *Life Force in the Great Pyramids.* Marina del Rey, CA: De Vorss, 1977.

Cross, J. L. *The Masonic Textbook.* New York: A. S. Barnes, 1857.

Cusick, D. *Ancient History of the Six Nations.* Lockport, NY: Niagara County Historical Society, 1824.

The Daily Graphic, "The Great Seal: The law of heraldry—the new die—valuable review." *The Daily Graphic,* May 14, 1885, 591.

Daniels, R. Personal correspondence between Rex Daniels and the author, March 14, 1974.

Davis, D. Some themes of counter subversion: An analysis of anti-Masonic, anti-Catholic, and anti-Mormon literature. In *Conspiracy, the Fear of Subversion in American History,* R. O. Curry and T. M. Brown, Eds. New York: Holt, Rinehart and Winston, 1972.

DeChardin, P. T. *Future of Man* (N. Denny, Trans.). New York: Harper & Row, 1964.

DeLubicz, R. A. S. *Symbol and the Symbolic* (R. Lawlor and D. Lawlor, Trans.). Brookline, MA: Autumn Press, 1978.

DeVos, C. *The Unfinished Work of the United States of America.* Coopersville, MI: New Age Publishing, 1921.

Dockstader, F.J. *The American Indian in Graduate Studies: A Bibliography of Theses and Dissertations.* New York: Museums of the American Indian, Heye Foundation, 1957.

Dolphin, L. T. Personal correspondence between Lambert T. Dolphin, senior physicist, SRI International, Menlo Park, CA, and the writer, April 2, 1979.

Douglas, L. Personal correspondence between Leslie Douglas and the writer, December 17, 1973, and February 12, 1974.

Doreal, M. *Symbolism of the Great Seal of the United States.* Colorado: Brotherhood of the White Temple, n.d.

Duncan, M. C. *Duncan's Masonic Ritual and Monitor.* Philadelphia: Washington Publishing, n.d.

Edinger, E. F. *Ego and Archetype.* Baltimore, MD: Penguin Books, 1973.

Edwards, E. E. The contributions of the American Indians to civilization. *Minnesota History,* 1934, *15*(3), 255–272.

Eliade, M. *Cosmos and History* (W. R. Trask, Trans.). New York: Harper & Row, 1959.

Feinstein, A. D. Personal mythology as a paradigm for a holistic public psychology. *American Journal of Orthopsychiatry,* 1979, *49*(2), 198–217.

Feinstein, A. D., and Krippner, S. *Personal Mythology.* Los Angeles: J. P. Tarcher, 1988.

Fell, B. *America, B. C.* New York: Wallaby, 1976.

Fell, B. *Bronze Age America.* Boston: Little, Brown & Company, 1982.

Fell, B. *Saga America.* New York: Times Books, 1980.

Fenton, W. N. A calendar of manuscript materials relating to the history of the Six Nations or Iroquois in depositories outside Philadelphia 1750–1850. *Proceedings,* American Philosophical Society, 1957, *97*(5), 578–595.

Fenton, W. N. Collecting materials for a political history of the Six Nations. *Proceedings,* American Philosophical Society, 1949, *93*(3), 141–158.

Fenton, W. N., Ed. *Parker on the Iroquois.* Syracuse, NY: Syracuse University Press, 1968.

Ferguson, I. M. *Heraldry and the U.S.A.* Vancouver: Association of the Covenant People, 1965.

Ferguson, M. *The Aquarian Conspiracy.* Los Angeles: J. P. Tarcher, Inc., 1980.

Flanagan, G. P. *Pyramid Power.* Glendale, CA: Pyramid Publishers, 1973.

Flanagan, G. P. *Pyramid Power II. Scientific Evidence.* Flagstaff, AZ: Flagstaff Vortex Industries, 1981.

Folger, C. F., & Snowden, A. L. *Relative to Striking a Medal Commemorative of the Adoption of the Great Seal of the United States.* Philadelphia: William F. Murphy's Son, 1885.

Forbes, J. *The Indian in America's Past.* Englewood Cliffs, NJ: Prentice-Hall, 1964.

Fosdick, S. *Nicholas Roerich.* Personal correspondence between Sina Fosdick, director, Agni Yoga Society and the writer, January 11, February 5, 14, 1974.

Fox, E. *The Historical Destiny of the United States.* New York: Church of the Healing Christ, 1937.

Frachtenberg, L. J. Our indebtedness to the American Indian. *Wisconsin Archaeologist,* 1915, *14*(2), 64–69.

Franklin, B. *The Autobiography of Benjamin Franklin.* New York: Macmillan, 1967.

Franklin, B. Journal of the Proceedings held at Albany in 1754. Massachusetts Historical Society Collections Third Series, 5, 5–74.

Franklin, B. *Poor Richard's Almanac for 1850.* New York: John Doggett, Jr., 1849.

Frankl, V. E. *Man's Search for Meaning: An Introduction to Logotherapy.* New York: Washington Square Press, 1965.

Frankl, V. E. Self-transcendence as a human phenomenon. *Journal of Humanistic Psychology,* 1966, *6*(2), 97–106.

Frankl, V. E. *The Will to Meaning: Foundations and Applications of Logotherapy.* New York: New American Library, 1969.

French, P. *John Dee—The World of an Elizabethan Magus.* London: Routledge and Kegan Paul, 1972.

Friedman, M. Aiming at the self: The paradox of encounter and the human potential movement. *Journal of Humanistic Psychology,* 1976, *16*(2), 5–34.

Fromm, E. *The Revolution of Hope.* New York: Harper & Row, 1974.

Fuson, R. H. *The Log of Christopher Columbus.* Camden, ME: International Marine Publishing Company, 1987.

Gardiner, A. *Egypt of the Pharaohs.* Great Britain: Oxford University Press, 1961.

Genzmer, G. H. Peter Miller. In *Dictionary of American Biography.* New York: Charles Scribner's Sons, 1933.

Goodavage, J. F. *Astrology: The Space Age Science.* New York: Signet Books, 1966.

Goodman, J. *American Genesis*. New York: Summit Books, 1981.

Gordon, C. *Before Columbus*. New York: Crown Publishers, 1971.

Graves, O. Benjamin Franklin as a Rosicrucian. *Rosicrucian Digest*, June 1938.

Haberman, F. *America's Appointed Destiny*. St. Petersburg, FL: New Kingdom Press, 1942.

Hall, M. P. *The Philosophy of Astrology*. Los Angeles: Philosophical Research Society, 1947.

Hall, M. P. *Man—The Grand Symbol of the Mysteries*. Los Angeles: The Philosophical Research Society, 1947.

Hall, M. P. *The Adepts in the Western Esoteric Tradition: Masonic Orders of Fraternity. Part IV*. Los Angeles: Philosophical Research Society, 1950.

Hall, M. P. *America's Assignment with Destiny, The Adepts in the Western Esoteric Tradition, Part V*. Los Angeles: Philosophical Research Society, 1951.

Hall, M. P. *The Phoenix*. Los Angeles: Philosophical Research Society, 1968.

Hall, M. P. *The Secret Destiny of America*. Los Angeles: Philosophical Research Society, 1972.

Hallowell, A. I. The backwash of the frontier: The impact of the Indian on American culture. In *The Frontier in Perspective*. Madison: University of Wisconsin Press, 1957.

Hallowell, A. I. The impact of the American Indian on American Culture. *American Anthropologist*, New Series, 1957, *59*(2), 201–207.

Hamaker, J. D. *The Survival of Civilization*. Burlingame, CA: Hamaker-Weaver Publishers, 1982.

Harley, L. R. *The Life of Charles Thomson*. Philadelphia: George W. Jacobs, 1900.

Harman, W. The societal implications and social impact of paranormal phenomena. In *Future Science*, J. White and S. Krippner, Eds. New York: Anchor Books, 1977.

Harman, W. Creative/intuitive decision-making: A new thrust for IONS. *Institute of Noetic Sciences Newsletter*, Summer 1979, *1*, 20–22.

Harman, W. Education for a transforming society. *Association for Humanistic Psychology Newsletter*, July, 1987, 19–22.

Harman, W. *Global Mind Change*. Indianapolis: Knowledge Systems, 1988.

Harris, A. William Barton. In *Biographical History of Lancaster County*. Lancaster: Elias Barr & Co., 1872.

Hayes, C. J. H. The American frontier—Frontier of what? *American Historical Review*, 1946, *51*(2), 199–216.

Heaton, R. *The Masonic Membership of Our Founding Fathers*. Silver Spring, MD: Masonic Service Association, 1965.

Heckethorn, C. *The Secret Societies*, Vol. 1. New York: University Books, 1966.

Heckewelder, J. *History, Manners and Customs of the Indian Nations Who Once Inhabited Pennsylvania and the Neighboring States*. New York: Arno Press, 1971.

Heindel, M. *The Rosicrucian Cosmo-Conception*. Oceanside, CA: The Rosicrucian Fellowship, 1956.

Heline, T. *America's Destiny, a New Order of Ages*. Oceanside, CA: New Age Press, 1941.

Heline C. *America's Invisible Guidance*. Los Angeles: New Age Press, 1949.

Herndon, S. M. Mr. Jefferson. *Rosicrucian Digest*, April 1961.

Hewitt, J. N. B. A Constitutional league of peace in the stone age of America: The League of the Iroquois and Its Constitution. National Anthropological Archives, Smithsonian Institution, Washington, DC, 1918.

Hewitt J. N. B. The founding of the League of the five nations by Deganawidah. National Anthropological Archives, Smithsonian Institution, Washington, DC.

Hieronimus, J. Z. Blowin' in the wind. *Baltimore Resources*, Fall, 1988.

Hieronimus, J. Z. Natural therapeutics: The role of the vital force. In *Current Management of Inflammatory Bowel Disease*, Theodore M. Bayless, M.D., Ed. Toronto: B. C. Decker, 1988.

Hieronimus, R. R. *Apocalypse Mural Guide*. Baltimore: Johns Hopkins, 1969, 1974.

Hieronimus, R. R. *Bicentennial Mural Guide*. Baltimore: Savitriaum, 1974.

Hieronimus, R. R. Were our Founding Fathers occultists? *Gnostica News*, *4*(9), part I. *4*(11), part II. St. Paul, MN: Llewellyn Publications, 1975.

Hieronimus, R. R. *The Two Great Seals of America*. Baltimore: Savitriaum, 1976.

Hieronimus, R. R. An historical analysis of the Reverse of America's Great Seal and its relationship to the ideology of humanistic psychology. Unpublished doctoral thesis. San Francisco, CA: Saybrook Institute, 1981.

Hieronimus, R. R. *Mythologies Expressed in the American Seal's Reverse*. Baltimore: The AUM Center, 1982a.

Hieronimus, R. R. *Psychology of the Talisman*. Baltimore: The AUM Center, 1982b.

Hieronimus, R. R. *The Growth Experience Depicted in the American Seal's Reverse*. Baltimore: The AUM Center, 1982c.

Hieronimus, R. R. *The 200th Anniversary of America's Great Seal*. Baltimore: The AUM Center, 1982d.

Hieronimus, R. R. *E Pluribus Unum*. Baltimore: The AUM Center, 1985a.

Hieronimus, R. R. *How to Pick Your Personal Winning Lottery Numbers*. New York: Crown Publishers, 1985b.

Hieronimus, R. R. Symbols: Agents through which consciousness is expressed in art. *Saybrook Review*, 1985c, *5*(2), 47–54.

Hieronimus, R. R. *Your Personal Winning Lottery Numbers*. New York: Warner Books, 1986.

Hoffman, E. *The Right to Be Human, a Biography of Abraham Maslow*. Los Angeles: J. P. Tarcher, Inc., 1988.

Houston, J. *The Search for the Beloved*. Los Angeles: J. P. Tarcher, 1987.

Hunt. G. *The Seal of the United States, How It Was Developed and Adopted*. Washington, DC: Department of State, 1892.

Hunt, G. *The History of the Seal of the United States*. Washington, DC: Department of State, 1909.

Hunt, G. The Seal. In *The Department of State of the United States: Its History and Function*. New Haven, CT: Yale University Press, 1914.

Huntington, E. *The Red Man's Continent: A Chronicle of Aboriginal America*. New Haven, CT: Yale University Press, 1921.

Iowa University Library. Personal correspondence between Earl M. Rogers and the writer, February 27, March 19, 25, 1974.

Israel House of David. *Washington's Vision, Strange Forecast of the Destiny of the American Nation.* Benton Harbor, MI: Israel House of David, n.d.

Jacobi, J. *Complex Archetype: Symbol in the Psychology of C. G. Jung.* Princeton, NJ: Princeton University Press, 1974.

Jahn, R. G., and Dunne, B. J. *Margins of Reality.* New York: Harcourt Brace Jovanovich, 1987.

James, G. W. *What the White Race May Learn from the Indian.* Chicago: Forbes & Co., 1908.

Jefferson, T. *The Life and Morals of Jesus of Nazareth.* New York: The World Publishing Company, 1942.

Johansen, B. E. *Forgotten Founders.* Boston: The Harvard Common Press, 1982.

Johnson, M. M. *The Beginning of Freemasonry in America.* Kingsport, TN: Southern Publishers, 1924.

Johnston, C. M., Ed. *The Valley of the Six Nations.* Toronto: University of Toronto Press, 1964.

Jung, C. G. *Two Essays on Analytic Psychology,* H. Read, M. Fordham, and G. Adler, Eds. (R. F. C. Hall, Trans.). Bollingen Series 20, Vol. 7. Princeton, NJ: Princeton University Press, 1953.

Jung, C. G. (V. S. de Laszlo, Ed.). *Psyche and Symbol.* New York: Doubleday, 1958.

Jung, C. G. *Symbols of Transformation,* H. Read et al., Eds. (R. F. C. Hull, Trans.). Bollingen Series 20, Vol. 5. Princeton, NJ: Princeton University Press, 1967.

Jung, C. G. *Four Archetypes: Mother, Rebirth, Spirit, Trickster* (R. F. C. Hull, Trans.). C. W. Bollingen Series 20, Vol. 9 (pt. 1). Princeton, NJ: Princeton University Press, 1970.

Jung, C. G. *Mandala Symbolism* (R. F. C. Hull, Trans.). C. W. Bollingen Series 20, Vol. 8. Princeton, NJ: Princeton University Press, 1973a.

Jung, C. G. *Synchronicity* (R. F. C. Hull, Trans.). C. W. Bollingen Series 20, Vol. 8. Princeton, NJ: Princeton University Press, 1973b.

Jung, C. G. *The Archetypes and the Collective Unconsciousness,* H. Read et al., Eds. (R. F. C. Hull, Trans.). C. W. Bollingen Series 20, Vol. 9, (pt. 1). Princeton, NJ: Princeton University Press, 1975.

Kaianerekowa. *The Great Law of Peace of the Longhouse People (Iroquois League of Six Nations)*. White Roots of Peace, Mohawk Nation at Akwesasne, 1971.

Kahn, D. *The Codebreakers*. New York: Macmillan, 1967.

Kennedy, A. *The Importance of Gaining and Preserving the Friendship of the Indians to the British Interest Considered*. New York: James Parker, 1751.

Kerényi, C., and Jung, C. G. Prolegomena. *Essays on a Science of Mythology* (R. F. C. Hull, Trans.). Bollingen Series 22. Princeton, NJ: Princeton University Press, 1969.

Kimm, S. C. *The Iroquois: A History of the Six Nations of New York*. Middleburgh, NY: P. W. Danforth, 1900.

Krajenke, R. K. Edgar Cayce and the metaphysical bicentennial. *The A.R.E. Journal*, 1976a, *11*(3), 1–4.

Krajenke. R. K. *The Psychic Side of the American Dream*. Virginia Beach, VA: A.R.E. Press, 1976b.

Krippner, S. The cycle in deaths among U. S. presidents elected at twenty year intervals. *International Journal of Parapsychology*, 1967, *9*, 145–153.

Krippner, S. *Song of the Siren*. New York: Harper and Row, 1977b.

Krippner, S., and Villoldo, A. *The Realms of Healing*. Millbrae, CA: Celestial Arts, 1976.

Kuhn, T. S. *The Structure of Scientific Revolutions*. Chicago: University of Chicago Press, 1970.

Landone, B. *Prophecies of Melchi-Zedek in the Great Pyramid and Seven Temples*. New York: Book of Gold, 1940.

Lang, C. R. The reverse side of the Seal of the United States and its symbolism. *Divine Life Magazine* (Chicago: Independent Theosophical Society of America), May 15, 1917, 1, 7, 18, 9.

Lannin, W. H. *The Great Seal of Our Nation*. Portland, ME: Smith & Sale, 1931.

Lawrence, R. B. *George Washington Plays*. Washington, DC: Washington's Bicentennial Commission, 1931.

Leadbeater, C. W. *The Hidden Life in Freemasonry*. Adyar, India: Theosophical Publishing House, 1963.

Lester, R. P. *Lester's Look to the East*. Danbury, CT: Behreus Publishing, 1927.

Lewis, H. S. *Rosicrucian Questions and Answers.* San Jose, CA: The Rosicrucian Press, 1941.

Lewis, H. S. The Great Seal of the United States. *The Rosicrucian Forum* (San Jose, CA: The Rosicrucian Order), February 1956, 90–92.

Lewis, H. S. *The Symbolic Prophecy of the Great Pyramid.* Kingsport, TN: Kingsport Press, 1964.

Locke, A., and Stern, B. J. Eds. *When Peoples Meet: A Study in Race and Culture Contacts.* New York: Hinds, Hayden, and Eldredge, 1946.

Lossing, B. J. The Great Seal of the United States. *Harper's New Monthly Magazine,* July 13, 1856, 178–186.

Mackey, A. G. *Revised Encyclopedia of Freemasonry,* 3 Vols. New York: Macoy Publishing and Masonic Supply, 1966.

Malone, D. *Jefferson and His Time, vol. 1. Jefferson the Virginian.* Boston: Little, Brown & Co., 1948.

Malone, D. *Jefferson and the Rights of Man.* Boston: Little, Brown, 1951.

Malone, D. *Jefferson and the Ordeal of Liberty.* Boston: Little, Brown, 1962.

Maslow, A. H. Comments on Dr. Frankl's paper. *Journal of Humanistic Psychology,* 1966, 6(2), 107–112.

Maslow, A. H. *Motivation and Personality,* 2nd ed. New York: Harper & Row, 1970.

Maslow, A. H. *Religious Values and Peak Experiences.* New York: Penguin Books, 1977.

Maslow, A. H. *The Further Reaches of Human Nature.* New York: Penguin Books, 1978.

May, R. *The Courage to Create.* New York: Bantam Books, 1976.

May, R. *The Meaning of Anxiety.* New York: Simon & Schuster, 1977.

Mishlove, J. *Psi Development Systems.* New York: Ballantine Books, 1983.

Morey, G. K. *The Seal of the United States, Its Message.* Quakertown, PA: Philosophical Publishing, 1923.

Morey, G. K. *Mystic Americanism.* New York: Eastern Star Publishing, 1924.

Morgan, E. S. *The Mirror of the Indian: An Exhibition of Books and Other Source Materials*. Providence, RI: The Associates of the John Carter Brown Library, 1958.

Morgan, L. H. *League of the Ho-de-no-sau-nee or Iroquois*. New York: Dodd, Mead & Co., 1902.

Morgan, W. T. The five nations and Queen Anne. *Mississippi Valley Historical Review*, 1927, *13*, 169–189.

Morse, S. *Freemasonry in the American Revolution*. Washington, DC: The Masonic Service Association of the United States, 1924.

Mosley, J. L. *The Great Seal of the United States of America*. Amherst, WI: Aquarian Age Research Society, 1974.

Murphy, G. *Personality: A Biosocial Approach to Origins Structures*. New York: Harper, 1947.

Musès, C., and Young, A., Eds. *Consciousness and Reality*. New York: Outerbridge and Lazard, 1972.

Neuman, E. *The Great Mother* (R. Manheim, Trans.). Bollingen Series 47. Princeton, NJ: Princeton University Press, 1970.

Neuman, E. *The Origins and History of Consciousness* (R. F. C. Hull, Trans.). Bollingen Series 42. Princeton, NJ: Princeton University Press, 1971.

Neuman, E. *Art and the Creative Unconscious*. (R. Manheim, Trans.). Bollingen Series 41. Princeton, NJ: Princeton University Press, 1974.

Newhouse, S. *Constitution of the Five Nations' Indian Confederation*. National Anthropological Archives, Smithsonian Institution, Washington, DC, 1880.

Newman, E. P. *The Early Paper Money*. Racine, WI: Whitman Publishing, 1967.

Noll, G., et al. Self-actualization, self-transcendence and personal philosophy. *Journal of Humanistic Psychology*, 1974, *14*(3), 53–73.

Odajnyk, J. W. *Jung and Politics*. New York: Harper & Row, 1976.

Orlandi, D., Ed. *The Life and Times of Washington*. New York: Curtis Publishing, 1967.

Osten, G. *The Astrological Chart of the United States*. Briarcliff Manor, NY: Stein & Day, 1976.

Parker, A. C. *The American Indian, the Government and the Country*. New York: New York Public Library, 1915.

Parker, A. C. *An Analytical History of the Seneca Indians*. Rochester, NY: Lewis H. Morgan Chapter, 1926.

Parker, A. C. The Constitution of the Five Nations. In *Parker on the Iroquois*, W. N. Fenton, Ed. Syracuse, NY: Syracuse University Press, 1968.

Patterson, R. S. *The Old Treaty Seal of the U.S.A.* Washington, DC: American Foreign Service Association, 1949.

Patterson, R. S. Seal of the United States. In *Encyclopedia Britannica*. Chicago: William Benton, 1971.

Patterson, R. S. *The Great Seal of the United States*. Washington, DC: Department of State Publication 8868, 1976.

Patterson, R., and Dougall, R. *The Eagle and the Shield*. Washington, DC: Department of State, 1976.

Patton, J. S. *Jefferson, Cabell and the University of Virginia*. New York: The Neal Publishing Company, 1906.

Pearce, R. H. *The Savages of America: A Study of the Indian and the Idea of Civilization*. Baltimore: Johns Hopkins University Press, 1965.

Pegler, W. The guru letters: Wallace meets the Roerich Cultists. *Newsweek*, March 22, 1948.

Penfield, M. *An Astrological Who's Who*. York Harbor, ME: Arcane Publications, 1972.

Perkins, L. *Masonry in the New Age*. Lakemont, GA: CSA Press, 1971.

Pike, A. *Morals and Dogma of the Ancient and Accepted Scottish Rite of Freemasonry*. Charleston: Southern Jurisdiction, F. M., 1906.

Pound. A. *Johnson of the Mohawks*. New York: Macmillan, 1930.

Preble, G. H. *History of the Flag of the United States of America*. Boston: A. Williams and Co., 1880.

Price, P. W. *The Great Seal: Key to Our Destiny*. New York: Exposition Press, 1952.

Progoff, I. *The Death and Rebirth of Psychology*. New York: Julian Press, 1969.

Progoff, I. *Depth Psychology and Modern Man*. New York: McGraw-Hill, 1973a.

Progoff, I. *Jung—Synchronicity, and Human Destiny*, 2nd ed. New York: Dell, 1973b.

Prophet, E. C., and Prophet, M. L. *Saint Germain on Alchemy*, Vol. 1. Livingston, MT: Summit University Press, 1987.

Puharich, A., Ed. *The Iceland Papers*. Amherst, WI: Essentia Research Associates, 1979.

Quaife, M. M., et al. The Seal of the United States. In *The History of the United States Flag*. New York: Harper & Row, 1961.

Quimby, G. I. *Indian Culture and European Trade Goods: The Archaeology of the Historic Period in the Western Great Lakes Region*. Madison: University of Wisconsin Press, 1966.

Raymond, E. *The Great Seal of America*. Aritson Sales, USA, 1979.

Read, H. *Icon and Idea*. Cambridge, MA: Harvard University Press, 1955.

Reaman, G. E. *Trail of the Iroquois Indians: How the Iroquois Saved Canada for the British Empire*. New York: Barnes & Noble, 1967.

Regardie, I. *My Rosicrucian Adventure*. St. Paul, MN: Llewellyn Publications, 1971.

Renn, B. Personal correspondence between Bernice Renn, Keeper of the Seal, U. S. State Department, and J'Nevelyn Terrell, January 8, 1980.

Richards, M. C. *Centering*. Middletown, CT: Wesleyan University Press, 1974.

Richards, A., and Richards, F. The whole person. *Journal of Humanistic Psychology*, 1974, *14*(3), 21–27.

Richardson, J. *Richardson's Monitor of Freemasonry*. Philadelphia: David McKay, n.d.

Robison, J. *Proofs of a Conspiracy*. Boston: Western Islands, 1967.

Roerich, N. *Realms of Light*. New York: Roerich Museum Press, 1931.

Roerich, N. Cultural unity. In *The Cochin Argus*. 319 W. 107th St., New York, 1943 (mimeographed article).

Rogers, C. R. *Client-Centered Therapy*. New York: Houghton Mifflin, 1965.

Root, E. *The Iroquois and the Struggle for America*. Address on the Tercentennial celebration of the discovery of Lake Champlain, Plattsburg, NY, July 7, 1909. Washington, DC: Sudworth Printing Company, 1909.

Rosicrucian Order. Personal correspondence between A. C. Piepenbrink, Supreme Secretary, Rosicrucian Order, San Jose, CA, and the writer, August 1, 1972.

Rubincam, M. A memoir of the life of William Barton, A. M. (1754–1817). *Pennsylvania History*, 1945, *12*(3), 179–193.

Sachse, J. F. *Benjamin Franklin as a Freemason*. Lancaster, PA: New Era Publishing, 1906.

Sachse, J. F. *Washington's Masonic Correspondence*. Lancaster, PA: New Era Printing Company, 1915.

Schlesinger, A. M. Liberty tree: A genealogy. *New England Quarterly*, 1952, *25*, 435–458.

Schlesinger, A. M. *The Age of Roosevelt: The Coming of the New Deal*. New York: Houghton & Mifflin, 1958.

Seiss, J. A. *The Great Pyramid: A Miracle in Stone*. New York: Rudolph Steiner Publications, 1973.

Singer, J. *Boundaries of the Soul*. Garden City, NY: Anchor Books, 1973.

Singer, J. *Androgyny*. Garden City, NY: Anchor Books, 1977.

Smyth, P. *Our Inheritance in the Great Pyramid*. London: William Isbister, 1880.

Sparks, J. *The Writings of Washington*, Vol. XI. New York: Harper & Brothers, 1848.

Speck, F. G. The Iroquois: A study in cultural evolution. Bloomfield Hills, MI: *Cranbrook Institute of Science Bulletin*, 1945, *23*.

Spence, L. *Encyclopedia of Occultism*. New York: University Books, 1968.

Spenser, R. K. *The Cult of the All-Seeing Eye*. Hawthorne, CA: Christian Book Club of America, 1968.

Stauffer, V. *New England and the Bavarian Illuminati*. New York: Columbia University Press, 1918.

Steinmetz, G. *The Royal Arch—Its Hidden Meaning*. New York: Macoy Publishing, Masonic Supply Co., 1946.

Strickland, E. D. *Iroquois Past and Present*. Buffalo: A.M.S. Press, 1901.

Swann, I. *Natural ESP*. New York: Bantam, 1987.

Taliaferro, A. A. The Great Seal of the United States. *The Rosicrucian Digest*, June 1972, 9–11, 33, 36.

Targ, R., and Harary, K. *The Mind Race: Understanding and Using Psychic Abilities*. New York: Villard Books, 1984.

Thomson, I. L. The Great Seal of the United States. In *Encyclopedia Americana*, Vol. 13. New York: American, 1962.

Tillich, P. *Dynamics of Faith*. New York: Harper and Brothers, 1958.

Tillich, P. *Systematic Theology*, Vol. III. Chicago: The University of Chicago Press, 1963.

Tompkins, P. *Secrets of the Great Pyramid*. New York: Harper and Row, 1971.

Tooker, E., Ed. *Iroquois Culture, History, and Prehistory: Proceedings of a Conference in Iroquois Research, Glens Falls, NY, 1965*. Albany, NY: State Education Department, 1967.

Toth, M., and Neilson, G. *Pyramid Power*. New York: Freeway Press, 1974.

Toth, M. *Pyramid Prophecies*. Rochester, VT: Destiny Books, 1988.

Totten, C. *The Great Seal of the United States, Its History and Heraldry*, Vols. 1 and 2. New Haven, CT: Our Race Publishing, 1897.

Trenchard, J. Description of the arms of the United States. *Columbia Magazine* (Philadelphia), September, 1786, 33–34.

Ullman, M., Krippner, S., and Vaughn, A. *Dream Telepathy*. New York: Macmillan, 1973.

Underhill, R. M. *Red Man's Continent: A History of the Indians in the United States*. Chicago: University of Chicago Press, 1953.

U.S. Department of State. *The Seal of the United States*. Department of State publication 1314, Washington, DC: U.S. Government Printing Office, 1939.

U.S. Department of State. *The Seal of the United States*. Department of State publication 2860, Washington, DC: U.S. Government Printing Office, 1947.

U.S. Department of State. *The Seal of the United States*. Department of State publication 6455, Washington, DC: U.S. Government Printing Office, 1957.

U.S. Department of State. *The Great Seal of the United States*. Washington, DC: U.S. Government Printing Office, 1970.

Valentine, T. *The Great Pyramid: Man's Monument to Man*. New York: Pinnacle Books, 1975.

Van Doren, C. *Benjamin Franklin*. New York: Viking Press, 1938.

Wadhams, A. *An Essay upon the Origin and Use of Seals, also Introducing a Design for an Improved Seal of the United States.* Albany, NY: Weare C. Little, 1865.

Waite, A. *The Brotherhood of the Rosy Cross.* New York: University Books, n.d.

Wallace, H. A. *America Must Choose.* New York: Foreign Policy Association & World Peace Foundation, 1934a.

Wallace, H. A. *Statesmanship and Religion.* New York: Round Table Press, 1934b.

Wallace, H. A. Personal correspondence between Wallace and Mr. Dal Lee, and Hon. George M. Humphrey, February 6, 1951 and December 10, 1955.

Wallace, P. A. W. The return of Hiawatha. *New York State History,* 1948, *39,* 385–403.

Waterman, E. In God we trust. *Rosicrucian Fellowship Magazine,* 1973, *65*(7), 294–297, 303.

Webster, N. *Secret Societies and Subversive Movements.* n.s.: Christian Book Club, n.d.

Weiser, C. *Narrative of a Journey from Tulpehocken in Pennsylvania to Onondago, the Headquarters of the Six Nations of Indians in 1737.* Philadelphia: J. Pennington, 1853.

West, J. A. *Serpent in the Sky.* New York: Harper & Row, 1979.

Whalen, W. *The Rosicrucians.* Chicago, IL: Claretian Publications, 1965.

Wiesenthal, S. *Sails of Hope: The Secret Mission of Christopher Columbus.* New York: Macmillan, 1973.

Williams, R. C. *Russian Art and American Money.* Cambridge, MA: Harvard University Press, 1980.

Wilson, A., and Shea, R. *Illuminatus: Part I, the Eye in the Pyramid.* New York: Dell, 1975.

Wilson, E. *Apologies to the Iroquois.* New York: Farrar, Straus & Cudahy, 1960.

Wilson, L. *The Coat of Arms: Crest and the Great Seal of the United States of America.* San Diego, CA: N. Francis Maw, 1928.

Wise, J. C. *The Legacy of Jefferson.* n.s.: by the author, n.d.

Wittemans, F. *History of the Rosicrucians.* London: Rider and Co., 1938.

Wright, J. G. *The National Identity of the United States with Manesseh*. Vancouver, Canada: British Israel Association, n.d.

Wyckoff, H. S. The Great American Seal. *The Mystic Light, the Rosicrucian Magazine*, n.d., 56–62.

Yates, F. A. *Giordano Bruno and the Hermetic Tradition*. Chicago: University of Chicago Press, 1979.

Yates, F. A. *The Rosicrucian Enlightenment*. London: Routledge and Kegan Paul, 1972.

Yates, F. A. *The Occult Philosophy in the Elizabethan Age*. London: Ark Paperbacks, 1983.

Young, A. *The Bell Notes*. New York: Delacorte Press, 1979.

Zieber, J. J. Charles Thomson, The Sam Adams of Philadelphia. *Mississippi Valley Historical Review*, 45(3), 1968, 464–480.

Index